The Oy of Sex

The Oy of Sex

Jewish Women Write Erotica

Edited by Marcy Sheiner

CLEIS
PRESS

Published in the United States by Cleis Press Inc., P.O. Box 14684, San Francisco, California 94114.

Printed in the United States.
Cover and Text Design: Scott Idleman/Blink
Cover Photo: Phyllis Christopher
Logo art: Juana Alicia
First Edition.
10 9 8 7 6 5 4 3 2 1

Notices of copyright and reprint permissions appear on page 220.

Library of Congress Cataloging-in-Publication Data

The oy of sex : Jewish women write erotica / edited by Marcy Sheiner.
   -- 1st ed.
      p.   cm.
   ISBN 1-57344-083-3 (alk. paper)
   1. Erotic stories, American. 2. Jewish women--Sexual behavior--Fiction.
   3. American fiction--Women authors. I. Sheiner, Marcy.
   PS648.E709   1999
   813'.01083538'082--dc21   99-11003
                                                                  CIP

Acknowledgments

Thanks to my publishers, Frédérique Delacoste and Felice Newman, for their enthusiasm and guidance; to Sandra Marilyn for her generous matronage; and to Joan Nestle for her decades of work on behalf of women.

Thanks to Corrinneshikel, Shoshana, and the rest of Mothertongue Theater for helping me solidify my Jewish identity; to Judith Linzer for her scholarly advice; and to my personal rabbi, Shar Rednour, who does what rabbis are supposed to do—figure out answers to ethical questions.

Thanks to the WELL online community for all their hilarious title suggestions, and in particular to the Jewish conference for their input about Judaism and sexuality as well as their helpful Yiddish definitions; to Andreas Ramos for sending me the Israeli personal ads; and to *Lilith* magazine for their help and support.

And a big round of applause for Miriam Wolf, who came up with the winning title.

For Andrea, my sexy Jewish soul sister

Contents

9   Introduction
       Marcy Sheiner

15   Nice Jewish Girls
       Susanna J. Herbert

25   The Gift of Taking
       Joan Nestle

30   The *Babka* Sisters
       Lesléa Newman

44   Bagels and Bialeys
       Gayle Brandeis

47   *L'Chaim*: A *Shiksa's* Story
       Carol Queen

53   Catholic Boys
       Harvest Garfinkel

70   Mother Was Right
       Judith Arcana

76   Shayna's *Shabbat*
       Claudine Taupin

85   One Single Night
       Susanna J. Herbert

95   *Shabbos Mitzvah* for a Jewish Princess
       Sara Leder

112   The Nanny of Ravenscroft
       Joyce Moye

124   Pierced
       Emma Holly

145   Out of Brooklyn
       Robin Bernstein

156   To Celebrate the Ordinary
       Elaine Starkman

160   The Locusts
       Cara Bruce

164   Linguistic
       Stacy Reed

178   Israeli Personal Ads
       From the Internet

184   From *He, She and It*
       Marge Piercy

194   The Feast of the Harvest
       Ariel Hart

205   From *Any Woman's Blues*
       Erica Jong

211   About the Authors

215   About the Editor

217   Glossary

I ntroduction

GENESIS

The idea for a book of erotic fiction by and about Jewish women had its genesis a few years ago, when I was writing an "Erotica Roundup" for the Valentine's Day issue of the *San Francisco Bay Guardian*. Plowing through boxes of anthologies generously loaned to me by the Good Vibrations library, I noticed themes ranging from fairy tale motifs to vampires, along with several ethnic collections. African Americans were represented by *Erotique Noire*, Asian Americans had *On a Bed of Rice*, and Latinas had *Pleasure in the Word*. I was immediately struck by the notable absence of sex writing specifically by Jews, particularly by Jewish women, arguably the most verbal ethnic group in America. Maybe, I rationalized, the heyday for Jewish women's writing had come and gone with the 1970s women's movement; still, Erica Jong's "zipless fuck" notwithstanding, that burst of confessional novels and feminist theory was for the most part devoid of explicit sex.

Having been around the erotica scene for a decade, I

knew that as many Jews as gentiles were writing the stuff—maybe even more. So why no collection?

JUDGES

Jews have always been subjected to nasty stereotypes, sexual and otherwise. Hitler labeled Jewish women pigs, and the Nazi regime perpetuated an image of Jews as lecherous pornmongers. Dirty Jew. Jewish Slut. Filthy Kike. The list goes on.

Perhaps Jews had been sufficiently silenced by such epithets. Maybe they were afraid that a collection of Jewish sex stories would feed ancient—and not so ancient—hatreds. Whatever the reason for the lack of a cohesive Jewish erotic sensibility, I decided to remedy the situation by providing a forum. Once I decided to do a book, though, I faced another rude awakening: when I began sending out calls for submissions and telling people I was putting together a collection of Jewish women's erotica, they invariably snickered and asked, "What's different about Jewish erotica?" Taken aback, I replied, somewhat apologetically, that I simply wanted stories by and about Jewish women; they may or may not be different; we'll see what they write. Even I didn't expect heavy Jewish content in the stories—but that is exactly what I got.

With one or two exceptions, the stories in this collection are heavily laden with Jewish symbols, holy days, customs, cultural references, and a hefty dose of Yiddish—so much, in fact, that I decided a glossary was necessary. Either my guidelines were interpreted literally, or there's a vast mine of Jewish custom and lore woven into our sexuality that's just been waiting for an opportunity to burst forth. To those who wondered what could possibly be distinct about Jewish erotica, *The Oy of Sex* is the beginning of an answer.

DEUTERONOMY

So what *are* the stereotypes that plague Jewish American women? Two of them are exemplified in the following joke: Q: How do you get a Jewish girl to stop fucking? A: You marry her.

This, one of my all-time favorite jokes, first heard when I was an adolescent, can be interpreted several ways. On the surface, it says that Jewish women only "put out" to get the brass, or gold, ring. On the other hand, it tells us, frankly, that Jewish girls like to fuck. Unburdened by the Christian admonitions against carnal pleasure, the Jewish girl is more likely to rejoice in her sensuality. This is, of course, a positive identity, one we can at last proudly claim. On the other hand, it feeds the stereotype of the Jewish girl as slutty.

The other half of the joke is the allusion to the JAP, the Jewish American Princess, the Sadie of *Funny Girl*, who wants her husband to "do for me, buy for me," the spoiled brat who remains untouchable lest her hair and makeup get out of whack.

Other stereotypes are even more unkind: Fat. Loud. Aggressive. Moneygrubbing. Unfeminine. The only some-what positive stereotype is the beloved Jewish mother, who cooks chicken soup by the gallon and bestows kindness upon one and all—but she is generally relegated to the kitchen and seen as an asexual frump.

And where in our cultural images do these stereotypes ever get contradicted? Certainly not by Fran Drescher's whining Nanny. Certainly not by her predecessors, Molly Goldberg and Marjorie Morningstar, Jewish mother and JAP, respectively. In *Talking Back: Images of Jewish Women in American Popular Culture*, edited by Joyce Antler (New England University Press, 1998), June Sochen points to

Sophie Tucker, Fanny Brice, Joan Rivers, Barbra Streisand, and Bette Midler as representatives of "three generations of Jewish women entertainers who operated as shrewd and funny observers of the battle between the sexes, the double standard, and sexuality." Tucker, in particular, "looked like Mother Earth and sang like a red-hot mama." Her *schtick* and her songs were full of double entendres. But huge, boisterous Tucker was not someone whom most contemporary Jewish women would wish to adopt as a role model.

CHRONICLES

The stories in this collection shoot stereotypes straight to hell. "The Nanny of Ravenscroft," in her bunny slippers and nightie, is a far cry from the trashy Nanny of television fame. *"The Babka Sisters"* defy images of asexual grandmothers. "*L'Chaim*," written by our token *shiksa*, praises the Jewish woman in ways that we could never do for ourselves.

If there is one stereotype about Jews that rings true, and that we willingly embrace, it's our vast capacity for humor. The protagonists in "Catholic Boys," "Mother Was Right," and "Out of Brooklyn" laugh at themselves and get the rest of us to laugh along with them. The "Israeli Personal Ads," which have been circulating on the Internet, are hilarious not by accident. Just finding a name for this collection produced a bevy of jokes from Jews and gentiles alike: suggestions included *A Mitzvah in the Night*, *Hugs and Knishes*, *My Davenatrix*, *The J-Spot*, *Matzoh Balling*, and *Chicken Soup for Your Pants*. *The Oy of Sex*, coined way back by editor Miriam Wolf of the *San Francisco Bay Guardian*, won by a landslide.

Another stereotype that holds true is the Jewish love of food: Though contemporary Jewish American women suffer greatly from body image angst, we love cooking and eating as much as our ancestors did. The women in these stories may bemoan their ample thighs or asses, but food is frequently simmering on their stoves and resplendent feasts adorn their tables, whether it's the breadstuffs in "Bagels and Bialeys," the vegetarian matzo ball soup in "Shayna's *Shabbat*," or the groaning board in "The Feast of the Harvest."

LAMENTATIONS

While many of these stories are lighthearted, others are dead serious. "The Gift of Taking" illuminates how body image affects our sexuality; "The Locusts" plumbs the depths of a particularly Jewish grief. "Nice Jewish Girls," zippy and contemporary, explores the underlying theme of Jewish women's resentment of Jewish men who take *shiksas* as trophy wives. And "The *Shabbos Mitzvah*," in which Judaic custom is almost seamlessly interwoven with the theme of dominance and submission, is a startling enlightenment.

Fleshy bodies, tempting food, forbidden liaisons, Jewish grief, internalized anti-Semitism, and a few compensating laughs—*oy guttinyu*, is that all there is? Is it true that being a Jew means suffering, even when it comes to sex?

SONG OF SONGS

Most emphatically, no. The female characters in these stories have a strong sense of their sexuality. They revel in their lusty passions, whether on a one-night stand or within a long-term marriage. They mightily enjoy sex, and they go after it themselves or heed the call when others come knocking.

Jewish tradition is steeped in physical joy, including sexual pleasure. God is believed to combine both masculine and feminine attributes, and sex is considered an earthly mystical union that reflects the greater holy mystery, an act of unity celebrating the divine. The Hebrew Bible's Song of Solomon, also called Song of Songs, is widely regarded as one of the most erotic, sex-affirming passages in all of literature:

> ...*Thy navel is like a round goblet, which wanteth not liquor; thy belly is like an heap of wheat set about with lilies:*
>
> *Thy two breasts are like two young roes that are twins...*
> *This thy stature is like to a palm tree, and thy breasts to clusters of grapes...*
>
> *Come my beloved, let us go forth into the field; let us lodge in the villages...*

While women in the Hebrew Bible are routinely exploited, banished and shamed, nowhere is it written that sex is a sin. In fact, making love on the weekly Jewish Sabbath is considered a *mitzvah*.

May all your sexual experiences be *mitzvahs*.

Marcy Sheiner
January 1999

ice Jewish Girls

Susanna J. Herbert

"Jewish girls are the world's best cocksuckers and everybody knows it."

I was assured of this factoid by my best friend, Rachel,
who considers it a fundamental truth, as basic as Torah.
This becomes somewhat ironic when you consider that
Rachel is a hard-core dyke who has never slept with a man
and "wouldn't touch a dick if it was attached to a gazillion-
dollar check from the Publisher's Clearing House."

I thought again of her words as I lapped an exquisite,
pearly drop of precum that hung, seemingly transfixed,
from the tip of David's chubby kosher cock. I was teasing
him; his ragged breathing inspired me to use my tongue and
cheeks and lips as slowly as possible to consume every inch
of his impatient erection. David made love the same way he
conducted business: thoroughly and with a ruthless deter-
mination to triumph. But when his cock was sucked his
façade crumbled and he reverted, once more, to the horni-
est fourteen-year-old boy in school. There was something
wild and terribly amusing about knowing my skills at fella-
tio could turn the clock back to 1972.

Now my mouth locked at the base of his shaft and sucked hard, from stem to stern, as if drinking in the world's juiciest popsicle on a hot summer day. He began to moan and squirm, crying jagged monosyllabic pleas not to stop, please don't stop, oh yes, there, no, yessss, oh yes, please, suck, please, please, suck, yes, god, oh god, oh oh god, please don't stop, don't...stop!

Never dreaming of stopping, I varied my pace and style, using my mouth to suck and fuck him into oblivion. My cunt became hotter, wetter, but there was no time to touch myself and I didn't want to dilute his absolute need of my mouth. I allowed myself to enjoy the hunger in my throbbing cunt, directing the sexual heat back onto his need and desire. I enjoyed his helplessness, and the power I felt from being so very much in control. I made my movements deliberate, unpredictable: running my tongue along his shaft one minute, nipping his head the next, then slathering his balls with the flat of my tongue. My mouth had become his lifeline, breathing sustenance into his loins as his gasps punctuated the night.

It was time. I used my hands to cradle his balls and then pump the base of his shaft while sucking him in deeper and deeper. My hands roamed to his lush, luscious ass. As his fleshy cheeks tightened in my grasp, the eruption began.

Warm, salty cream filled my mouth, bathed my inner cheeks. I milked him, swallowing every drop, as he babbled rapturous incoherence. He pulled me to him and held me tightly, still the sweet innocent. He kissed me hungrily and we fell into a deep sleep. When we awoke some time later, in place of the boy, forty-year-old David had re-emerged, eager and able to make me come, but too neurotic to enjoy it.

After fucking me to climax (with stops en route for the

requisite fingering and pussy-licking), he kissed me nervously—worlds away from the burning embraces we had shared when his cock was hard—and repeated the confession that had become his postcoital mantra: "You know, I never fuck Jewish women." He said this proudly, as if somehow I should be grateful that he was making an exception in my case.

I asked him why he had such arbitrary prejudice against Jewish women. I expected his reply to be angry or defensive. It was condescending.

"Come on. Jewish women are so...so...*Jewish!*"

"And that means what?"

"Loud. Unattractive. Obnoxious. You know."

I pulled on my sweater and jeans. "I'm going home."

"Look, I don't mean you. You're really hot. You're not one of those women."

I was getting angrier. "I am, actually. And proud of it."

"Now you're pissed off. That's so Jewish."

"Good-bye, David."

I drove home trying to figure out just how and why we had become the enemy. Where did all that anger come from? How had Jewish women become the poster girls for the sexless, shopaholic, castrating shrew? Why did every Jewish man on TV have a blonde wife?

Rachel let me vent on the car phone, then offered more gospel. "Jewish women are brilliant in most things, but when it comes to their hearts, they give too much and men screw them over. You want to talk history? Ruth? Leah? Let's talk Adam. He keeps his first wife out of the story completely and gives the second one creation's first eating disorder." Her theology was original, to say the least.

"You're an accomplished, self-sufficient, beautiful

woman, bla bla bla," she continued, "but the bottom line is you're the quintessential Nice Jewish Girl. There is nothing better than that. Hell, I only fuck Nice Jewish Girls. But these guys don't want to see you for who you are. They need some bullshit Fran Drescher stereotype to justify their own cultural self-loathing. Why do you put up with that crap? You need to trash this guy from your database instantly. It's time to ask yourself if the fucking you're getting is worth the fucking you're getting."

Rachel always made me think, but what struck me now was the word "self-loathing." How much of my attraction to these men stemmed from our shared humor and cultural frame of reference—and how much of it justified my own insecurities and self-doubt?

When I was eight, the ideal woman was Twiggy. By the time I started to notice boys, their wet dreams starred Farrah Fawcett. It didn't take me long to realize that, as different as these two women were, I was nowhere near either of them on the physical continuum. Whereas the current ideal could go from cool British waif to sun-drenched California babe, the template was always some shade of Blonde Goddess. Despite the fact that I was blessed with a great body and a good mind, I never felt I measured up to what men found attractive. And so I sought out Jewish boys who saw me as one of the guys. (I did know girls who went the peroxide and plastic surgery route, but that wasn't my style. God bless Barbra for keeping her nose!)

And sexually? I made sure I was the hottest fuck on the block. Spent my puberty poring over everything from Dr.

David Reuben to Xaviera (yes, she was Jewish). I scrutinized *Penthouse* letters the way Yentl studied Talmud: devoutly and behind closed doors. I practiced kissing on pillows and fellating on bananas. My goal was not promiscuity but perfection. When a man was with me, I was going to fuck him out of any desire for those fantasy girls. My pleasure came from driving him wild. My need was to be needed, to be the mirror reflecting his insatiable orgasm.

I came home to the simplest and most impersonal form of end-of-the-millennium interaction: e-mail. I recognized David's online nickname, "BigMacher," and his unsubtle usage of *Yiddishkite* set the tone for his communiqué:

"Listen, I can't do this any more. You are way too real and I can't handle that right now. Thanks for the great fucking."

"Thanks for the great fucking?" Sheesh! Rejection never surprises me, but I'm always fascinated by its many shadings.

You can't cry when you've been dumped by someone you should've dumped first. Too embarrassing. You have to do something concrete. Positive.

I finished my comic novel, read the collective works of Phillip Roth and Cynthia Ozick, watched *The Way We Were* three times in a row (with a box of Kleenex and a pint of low-fat Ben & Jerry's for each viewing), gave up men, obsessed about men, did five hours a week at the gym, masturbated my brains out, lost nine pounds, and organized a lunch to which I invited every Nice Jewish Girl in my rolodex.

Together we tried to make sense of the Men of Our Tribe and why they either avoided us completely or played Advance/Retreat. Deborah blamed it on Nice Jewish Boy Freud, who helped make mothers the scapegoat for all things horrific. Rebecca cited the almost century-old image of women in popular culture, created by the Jewish founding fathers of the studio system: the Zanucks, Goldwyns, and Mayers, who left Russia so eager to assimilate that they created an on-screen America populated by blonde vixens and kindly Protestant mothers. Hannah cited recent studies that claimed Jewish men were rejecting the values of their fathers, foregoing the familial spiritual through-line personified by the Matriarch. Yael summed it up thusly: "Guys like bimbos. That ain't us."

The discussion was as stimulating as my personal life wasn't.

And then I met Paul, a meeting inadvertently precipitated by David. One Friday afternoon I was taking a long, solitary walk on the Third Street Promenade. Weaving my way through the trendy shops, slacker boutiques, and street mimes, I saw a pushcart vendor selling the most glorious tulips, each colossal bulb as big as my hand. As I approached to buy myself a bunch, I heard a voice squeal, "Oooh, Davy, get me the pink ones, puh-leeze!"

I looked around and there was David, accompanied by a Pamela Lee clone with legs up to her breasts. He spotted me and turned as pale as her neo-Yardley lip gloss. He stammered out that they'd just come from the nearby Santa Monica courthouse, where he was handling "Julie's" divorce. I was wracking my brain for a brilliant bon mot when a smooth, deep Kentucky drawl cut the awkward silence.

"There you are, darlin', " he said, looking me straight in the eye. "Ah thought ah'd lost you." He handed the florist a jumble of bills, plucked a lavish bouquet, and placed it in my arms. Both David and I checked out this stranger. He was tall, well over six feet, with eyes the color of morning sky and shaggy blonde hair as thick as honey. He was gorgeous, he'd appeared from nowhere and together we walked off, as David watched in rapt fascination.

We ducked around the corner into a tiny bistro, and before I could speak, he apologized.

"Ah'm sorry. Ah had no business doin' that. You must think Ah'm crazy. Ah just have this instinct, sometimes. My mama says it's psychic. It looked like you weren't too happy to run into him, so Ah just thought...Apologies for buttin' in."

"No. It was very sweet of you. And these flowers are gorgeous." I giggled, thinking of David's face. This fascinating stranger read my mind once more and revealed a dangerously intoxicating smile.

"He did look a right fool. He doesn't deserve you."

I found myself blushing. In a millisecond my mind's eye saw myself thanking him, excusing myself gracefully, and running to my car like a frightened wildebeest. But two hours later we were still in the café, laughing and lingering over glasses of Merlot. Over lunch I'd learned that Paul owned a ranch one hundred miles outside of Louisville, where he bred Arabian thoroughbreds and Tennessee Walkers. This was his first time in L.A., where he knew no one. Without asking, he got me to divulge the plot of my novel, my guilty pleasure of belting Beatles songs in the shower, my impersonation of Robert Duvall as Tom Hagen in *The Godfather Part II*, and my secret recipe for cranberry bread.

Shortly thereafter we were in his hotel suite, listening to the pounding Pacific surf, while he ran a blood-red tulip along my naked body. The soft petals tickled the lips of my wet, slippery cunt. Paul placed my hands above my head, then moved down to split my lips with his hungry tongue, having used the sinewy muscle to snake a determined path along my body, from mouth to neck to breasts, belly, and cunt. The room was spinning, as much from the sensation of his lips on my clit as from the surrealism of the situation. This was not a typical Nice Jewish Girl experience—at least for *this* NJG.

His body was smooth and hard, his pubic hair the color of burnished copper. His thick cock glistened, the head awash in precum. I longed to lap it clean, but he had other ideas. In fact, nothing followed my usual game plan. While I was used to orchestrating sex, he seemed more determined to touch than be touched. Any attempts I made to hold or suck him resulted in a sensual stroke or caress that made me collapse in a writhing heap. Wouldn't he vanish if I didn't give my all just to please him? Apparently not. He was too busy driving me into a hedonistic frenzy.

My ass rose off the bed, lifted involuntarily by the sensations from his fingers and tongue. It wasn't as simple as physical domination. He *willed* me to submit, thereby conducting my absolute pleasure.

A technicolor petal from the enormous tulip had dropped onto my mons. He pulled the remaining petals off one by one and scattered them over my burning flesh. All that remained was the blossom's sturdy stem. Playing to his sly rhythm, I bucked my throbbing pussy toward the hand that held the naked flower. My mouth was open, my breathing wet and heavy. He smiled and ran the stalk along my slit. I reached for it with my cunt, but he pulled it away. Before I could move, or ask, or beg, or plead, he swooped down and sucked hard on my breast. As this glorious sensation of pleasure tinged with pain washed over me, he thrust the thick stem into my cunt. He sucked harder on my breast and pinched my other nipple between his calloused thumb and forefinger. My jagged moans grew louder, although the pounding of my heart probably drowned out my verbal noises.

Fucked by a flower, flowering to this fantastic fuck—my thoughts and emotions swirled together like a design from one of those silly, splendid spinning paint machines at the school carnival. Once more Paul's mouth pressed against my inflamed cunt, kissing it, fucking it. I fingered my throbbing breast, knowing the globe would sport a purplish bruise within minutes. I delighted in the vision I would later explore in my bedroom mirror. What other marks would he paint on my body's canvas? As I rocked on the soft hotel bed, I relived each touch, even as he raised the seismic stakes by slowly inserting his middle finger up my ass.

My clit was liquid heat, a throbbing buoy in a sea of exploding cunt. God, I loved how he made me feel. His eyes never left mine, and in them I could see a gleam of satisfaction. I clutched the wooden post of the bed and began to come. The explosion traveled across my flesh. I closed my eyes as waves rocked my body, again and again. I moaned, I climbed, I crawled. I steamed, shook, and then exploded into his mouth, onto his hands and across his hot, steamy flesh.

He held me tightly, and as I continued to come he surprised me yet again by thrusting his torrid cock into me. I wrapped my arms around him and came and fucked and fucked and came. This wild electricity continued until we both screamed and fluttered and fell, into and around each other.

Bathed in perspiration, I softly kissed his lips, licked his rough, tender fingers. He ran the back of his hand lightly across my cheek.

"What a beautiful woman you are."

I said nothing. Where had he come from? He was so different from any man I had ever known. Truth be told, he was unlike any man I would have allowed myself to know. I would justify my prejudice by telling myself he would have rejected me as being too different. In my mind he would fall victim to those same cultural stereotypes, leaving him unable to see me. How wrong I was! And even so, I had no idea just how wrong I was.

My thoughts were interrupted by Paul's soothing drawl.

"Will you spend the weekend with me? Ah don't want to lose you. Ah want to know you better. And Ah sure as hell want to make you come about a million more times."

I erased my mental day planner and said I would gladly stay—but he would have to let me give as well as take. I was dying to show him a few of my tricks. He smiled.

"So we'll stay here. Ah'll order food and anything else you need and...oh, shit!"

"What's the matter?" I asked, suddenly envisioning a wife and three kids flying in from the South.

"There is one thing Ah have to do tonight. Maybe you'll join me?"

"What is it?" I asked. He looked embarrassed.

"Ah have to go to *shul*."

If I hadn't been lying down, I would have fallen down. "Excuse me?"

"Synagogue. Ah'm sorry. I thought you might be Jewish, too. Have you ever been to Friday-night services?"

You want to talk about misguided cultural assumptions? I threw my arms around Paul and laughed and laughed.

"What's so funny, darlin'?"

"Everything! Everything is gloriously, fabulously funny!"

So our weekend began.

The Gift of Taking

JOAN NESTLE

I walk into the room. She stands with her back to me, a large woman dressed for business. She turns to me: "I have been waiting." I need to know my arrival is important to her. She approaches me. "I will do what you want. I will do it better than you have ever had it done, and you will give me everything there is in you to give. You will pour it out on my hands, and I will hold you open." I love her for those words, for her knowledge of what I need and her caring enough to do it. We are alone in this room, having left outside all our accomplishments, all our other powers.

Here we will face each other, naked and yet dressed in ritual recognition. We will have the courage to bring to the surface the messages the body carries from older days. Here the daily camouflage of acceptable activity will be dropped. My submission in this room with this woman is my source of strength, of wisdom. It informs all my abilities in the other world, but here I can give it time to breathe its own air, to break the surface and show its own face.

There is a table in the room with sharp square edges. It looks uncomfortable, but I long for the feel of its edges against my back.

I am wearing a long dress that hides my body, my body
that I have hated so long for not being lean, hard: hated for
its flesh, thighs without tight muscles, large buttocks mocked
for many years but with a hunger all their own; and now
yearning for penetration by this woman's hand, her erotic
acceptance that will free me from the crime of being a big-
assed woman. I know this woman, my friend, will bring my
body to light, will make me use it and hear it, will strain it to
its fullest, and she will help me through her demands and her
pleasure to forget self-hatred. Through her gift of taking, I
will be given back to myself, a self that must live in this body
and thus desperately needs reconciliation.

"Come here, Joan."

I do, my eyes caught on hers, a blush spreading fire on
my face. "You must be ready for me before I touch you. I
want to feel your wetness waiting for me. You know that." I
do. She kisses me hard, her hands gripping my arms. The
force of her tongue pushes my head back. She stands back
and just looks at me. Her hands stay on me, and they will
throughout our time together.

My breasts have grown hard and she knows it. She
caresses my nipples, her eyes never leaving mine. "I want
them harder." My body hears, and I feel flesh change its own
form. Her fingers squeeze my nipples, but I do not drop my
eyes. The pain is sweet; it destroys the years of numbness. I
want her to squeeze harder. The message is exchanged in
silence, and her hands take fuller command of my breasts.
After a few minutes, I put my hand over hers to stop her giving. I can no longer hold my position.

"Now we will see."

She holds my head back as she slips her hand under
my dress. I tremble, trying to hold my thighs together,

knowing she will not allow me. She feels the wetness before she touches my underpants. My thighs have seeped their own waters. Her hand forces my legs further apart and her fingers push aside the fabric. "That is good, Joan," she says, as my wetness bathes her fingers. She curves the material into a ribbon and pushes it between my cunt lips, gliding her thumbnail over the wet curve. "You are a powerful woman, aren't you? Women listen to your words, and you do important work, but here you are in my hands." Her hand spreads my lips apart.

"Yes, yes."

She moves me closer to the table. She is ready to assume her full power, and I am ready to give to her. She holds me, undoes my dress. It falls open, and I feel the first shame of revelation, the fear she will turn away from me, from this body. "Good," she says. I hold on to her and close my eyes. I will not open them again until we are finished, but my hands will see her. I grip her shoulders, pulling her to me. She kisses me, deep, hard, forcing my mouth open. I take her tongue in, sucking on it, trying to hold it. She drops her head and sucks on my nipples, biting them. My nipples swell with fullness. She works harder. I know I will have marks to carry with me and I want them. I want to be reminded in the daily world of this breakthrough. The sweet soreness will burn through my heavy layers of work clothes and remind me of this need and this caring. I will blush with pleasure in the subway, or at a meeting, as a change in my body's position forces me to remember the time of openness.

Her hands are hard on me, and I want them to be. I hear her breath coming quicker and my own moaning breaking in and out. My hips move. I want her all inside of me. She pulls me back. For a brief moment I open my eyes. I can smell my sex in the room. "Your body is bursting with want."

"I know." I can see it, hear it, smell it. My body is covered with a dark flush, and I am moving with want. I want to scream out to her, "Now, please take me now," but I can't, even in this dream. Perhaps next time I will be able to scream. I want to. For so many years I have not screamed, for so many years the world was not safe enough, or there was no one there to hear it.

I close my eyes again as she moves toward me. She speaks to me, always calling to me, challenging me, forcing me to be there, and the force of her tells me she is there, caring and fighting for me. Her lips move against my cheeks as she puts her hand on me. Her fingers tear away the fabric. She takes me into her hand, pushing, squeezing, opening. She slips one finger into me. I gasp at how she fills me with that one thrust when I have taken so much and will again, but still the first entry has all the joy, the surprise of her power. "Open Joan, open, take me in. Maybe you can't. Maybe I'm too much for you." I hold on to her tighter, open more open to splitting to show her I can give a home to all she can give me. I can match her demanding with my giving, her hand with my insides. I speak to her through my muscles and my wetness. She moves in and out and I follow her. The table edge is cutting into my back as her weight pushes me over. She forces more fingers into me, and I feel as if I could take her whole hand, her arm. My hunger grows as she pushes against me, always talking to me, telling me she is there and wanting me.

I take her all in, throwing my whole body against her, repeating in a small deep voice, "Yes, I can do it. I can do it." Over and over again. She is a total force over me, and yet all her power is giving me myself. I know I am coming:

all the need, the fear, the loneliness has slipped down around her fingers, and she pulls at them as she moves me. I am all in that place where her hand has found entrance.

I come on her fingers, contract and hold her inside of me. She feels me and whispers, "There is more. I am not letting you go yet." She moves around inside of me, making my body flinch with more comings. All my strength is in my hands, my arms embracing her strength, feeling her shoulder move with the power of her entries. I fall back on the table; my head drops back and she begins to leave me. I know it will not be easy; I have locked around her fingers, and she must carefully break the grip of my body's gratefulness.

When my strength returns, I will thank her by kneeling in front of her and taking her wetness in my mouth. I will hold her legs strong against me, my breasts holding her up, and I will slowly, carefully, wisely—using my tongue's tip and its wide surface and my teeth and the power of my mouth—give to her my love and her pleasure.

The *Babka* Sisters

Lesléa Newman

Sit down, *shah*, you ready, you got your tin can going there, you want to make a test, make sure my voice is good, everything is working all right? Okay, so now I'm gonna tell you a story, a story I never told nobody, why I'm telling you, a stranger, I don't even know, but all right, *nu*, it's time.

Once upon a time, a long, long time ago, around the Stone Age it was, *takeh*, I was a young *maidl*, and quite a looker I was, too. I know what you're thinking, you look at me now and what do you see, a fat old lady wrinkled like a prune danish with hair like cotton candy, but *nu*, I had quite a shape in those days, my hair I wore in a braid down my back thick as a man's arm, my skin was smooth as a baby's *tuchus*, you don't believe me but you wait, *mamela*, gravity ain't got no favorites, it catches up to everyone, someday even you.

So my childhood ain't nothing to talk about, an ordinary girl I was, I went to school, I came home, I helped my mother with the housework, sure, five children she had, four boys and me, so who else is gonna help her? I had friends, too, boys and girls, no one special, there was like a group of

us that stuck together, to the movies we went, and to get a
nosh at the diner, dancing once in a while, you know we did
all the things that young people do.

And then, when I was sixteen, a new girl moved into
the neighborhood, and that girl, I had such a feeling for, I
just couldn't take my eyes from her. You know the expression "love at first sight," sure, who doesn't, well of course
that's what it was, but what did I know, we was two girls,
girls don't fall in love with girls, who ever heard of such a
thing? I just knew I wanted to be her friend, help her out,
you know, show her around, it could be overwhelming, such
a place, to a person who first walks in and don't know from
it, *nu*, it takes a while to get used to, it was a very big school.

Look, here's a picture of her, my Evie, you see, here we
are both in the last row, that's our class picture from
eleventh grade, we was both tall girls, now I'm all stooped
over like an old turtle, but back then my back was straight
as a *Shabbos* candle, from my posture my mother was
always proud. Ain't she gorgeous, my Evie? Look at that
dark, curly hair, black as midnight it was, Medusa I used to
call her, *nu*, it was that hair that started the whole thing.
Dark, curly hair and blue eyes, very unusual for a Jew, but
I swear her eyes were as blue as mine are brown, you can
see, under the cataracts my eyes are dark like coffee you
drink when there's no milk in the house. And could she fill
out a gymsuit, my Evie! Listen, years ago, no girl wanted to
be skinny, like sticks all you girls are now, what do they call
them the supermodels there, *feh*, one puff of wind could
knock them right down. We used to laugh at girls like that,
girls with no hips, no *tuchus*, we used to feel sorry for them,
the poor things.

So where was I? Oh, Evie, of course, Evie. The first

day I saw her, she was in the lunchroom sitting all by herself, *takeh*, and I was ashamed, a whole school, maybe five hundred boys and girls, maybe a thousand, and not one person held out a hand, nobody said, "You must be lonely, here, I'll sit with you, I'll talk to you, I'll show you where to take your tray." And blind they all was, they couldn't see this was no ordinary girl, this girl was something special, a gift from God she was, and nobody could see what was sitting there right before their very eyes?

So I got my sandwich, egg salad I got, and a carton of milk, and I brought my *tuchus* over and put it down on the seat right next to her.

"How do you do? I'm Ruthie," I said and that's when I knew I was lost, when I looked for the first time into those eyes. Like diamonds they twinkled, like stars, like the sun dancing on the ocean in a million pieces, all that and more was shining in my Evie's eyes.

"I'm Evie," she said. "How do you do?" And I couldn't even answer her, my voice was gone, on a trip it went, a vacation all of a sudden it took, I couldn't find it, so I went to take a drink of milk, but I was so nervous, can you believe it, I started to choke. And to make things worse, Evie clapped me on the back, and when I felt her hand touch me, even through my sweater and my blouse, I felt a charge, like a jolt, like I just put instead of the plug my finger in the socket, God forbid, but I swear, sure as I'm sitting here, it's true. And Evie was so concerned, she looked at me, so serious.

"Are you all right?" she asked, and all I could see were those two eyes above me, blue as the sky, like God finished making the heavens and he had a little fabric left over and decided the only thing left to do is make those little bits of heaven into Evie's eyes. Finally I got hold of myself and we ate our lunch and had a conversation, about what I couldn't tell you, whatever young girls talk about, school and families, this and that; whatever she said, I don't think I heard a word, I was too busy drowning in those blue, blue eyes.

Evie and I became fast friends after that. Every day we ate lunch together, every day together we walked home from school, Evie lived around the corner from me, how lucky could I get, I began to think maybe after all I did shine a little bit in God's eyes. Sometimes we'd study at her house, sometimes we'd study at mine, we became like part of each other's families, I would eat supper by her, she would eat supper by me, the *Babka* Sisters my mother used to call us, you know what *babka* is, darling, a dessert so sweet, with cinammon they make it sometimes, sometimes with chocolate, Evie and I loved it, we ate it all the time, so my mother gave us like a nickname, you know, like a joke. "Look who's here, the *Babka* Sisters," she'd say after school when we rang the bell.

Sometimes we'd have sleep-over dates, too. It was nothing unusual, all the girls did in those days. Evie would sleep over my house, I had my own room, not that we was so rich but because it ain't nice, a girl can't sleep with her brothers, so what could my mother do? Evie had a sister, Shirley her name was, and they shared one room, two beds they had, two dressers, two desks, everything matching you know, except the two girls, they didn't match so good, they was different as day and night, they used to fight like cats and dogs, so over to our house Evie came, every chance she could get.

So where was the boys, I bet you're thinking, two teenage girls, gorgeous like we was and neither of us had a fella? Me, the boys was never interested in, I was too much of a tomboy for them, my mother used to wring her hands and say, "Ruthie, take little steps, why do you have to walk like a truck?" And Evie, I think the boys were afraid of her, so beautiful she was, and so smart, she beat them by a mile, and then they'd have to get past me of course to get near her, we was always together and I wouldn't let them so easily by.

Sometimes when Evie and I were up in my room studying, I'd watch her out of the corner of my eye, so gorgeous she looked studying or writing, or just chewing her pencil. If she glanced up, I'd look away quickly, but once in a while, I'd meet her gaze. And sometimes I caught her staring at me, too.

"What?" I'd say, feeling kind of nervous, though I didn't know why.

"Nothing," Evie would answer with a shrug and a smile.

One night Evie was sleeping over, it was *Shabbos* I remember, my mother had made such a beautiful supper: her *matzo* ball soup that she was famous for all up and down the avenue, and fresh *challah* from the bakery and a roasted chicken, we was so full, we was busting after, such a feast it was. Evie and I helped my mother with the supper dishes and then we first had coffee and *babka*, no matter how stuffed we was we always had room for *babka*, and then we went up to my room. Evie had been a little quiet that night, and a few times I caught her staring at me across the supper table, but I didn't ask no questions, I figured if she had something to tell me, she'd tell. She looked a little moony that night, and I was only afraid she shouldn't tell me she had a crush on a fella, she couldn't spend so much time with me now, on dates she was gonna go out, and believe me if that's what Evie was going to say, I wasn't in a big hurry to find out.

Evie went into the bathroom to get undressed like she always did, and I got undressed as well. We both wore long, white nightgowns, cotton they were, everybody did back then. I turned off the light, lifted back the covers, and got into bed. It was dark, but not so you couldn't see, the moon shone right in my window, I still remember, it was full that night. Like a spotlight it was, shining down on Evie when she came back to my room, like a movie star she looked, I remember, there was something different about her, and then I realized what it was: instead of in a braid, all her hair, all those thick, black waves, was loose and hanging down.

"Ruthie, will you brush my hair?" Evie asked, her voice slow and thick and dreamy, and when I climbed out of bed and went to her, my movements were slow and dreamy, too. I took the brush from Evie's hand and stood behind her in the moonlight, brushing her hair from the crown of her head all the way down to her tiny, tiny waist. Up and down my hands went, brushing her hair for hours it seemed, days maybe, long after the last knot was untangled, long after her hair shone like a wet, black stone. Hypnotized I was, like a spell I was under, I couldn't move a muscle except for my arms, which couldn't stop brushing, brushing. I only wanted that moment to never end, me, Evie, the hairbrush, the moonlight, if I died right then and there I wouldn't be sorry, because I had already tasted a bit of heaven. But thank God my time wasn't up, for what happened after that I wouldn't have missed for anything: Evie turned around, the hairbrush clattered down from my hand, and before I even knew what was happening, there she was, my girl in my arms.

"Ruth," she whispered, and her mouth was so close to mine, I could feel her sweet breath on my skin and I breathed it in, wanting every part of her. "Ruth," she said again—not Ruthie, Ruth, like my name was holy, a prayer that could be answered only with her name, "Evelyn," like the song of the nightingale it was, so sweet on my lips. "Evelyn," I said again, "Evelyn." "Ruth," she answered and then she put her mouth on top of mine, and then we didn't say no more.

Her lips, how can I describe her lips, sweeter than *challah* they were, sweeter than *babka*, and soft, so soft, I was almost afraid if I licked them they would dissolve on my tongue, they would melt away like water. When Evie kissed me, the world as I had always known it came forever to an end, and a new world, a world so sweet, so fine, so holy and precious took its place instead.

It was Evie who broke that kiss and led me to the bed, the same bed we had slept in together for so many nights, but like *Pesach*, I knew this night would be different from all other nights, I knew there would be no nightgowns that evening to separate flesh from flesh. Evie was so confident, so unashamed, so proud, *takeh*, of her feelings for me, that I wasn't even afraid. She took my hands and put them on her breasts and I gasped at their softness, their firmness, their ripeness, so smooth and white her breasts were, her nipples so hard and rubbery and sweet, I swooned to take them under my tongue.

What, so surprised you are that an old woman like me should talk so, all you young girls with your blue hair and pierced eyebrows, up there at the university in your women's history class, you think there was no such girls in my time, you think you're the first, you think maybe you invented it? Well I've got news for you, there's more to tell, so either turn your tin can off and I'll keep still, or put your eyes back in your head, sit back, and listen.

Now then, I'll never forget that night as long as I live. So gentle Evie was, but so fierce, too, like a *Vildeh Chayah*, you know what that means, like a wild little beast.

"Here," she said, putting my hand where it never went before. "Harder," she said, "lower. Like this," and she put her hand on top of mine and showed me what to do. Where she learned such things, I didn't know, I didn't want to know, what did I care, all I wanted was to hear her breath coming hard and fast against my ear, her little cries of "*Oy, oy, oy,*" and then "Ruthie, my Ruthie, and then just "yes, yes, yes," oh how she crooned as my hands went up and down, in and out, all over her, my Evie who trembled, and shook, and yelped so loud I was only afraid my mother shouldn't come in, and then finally fell back against the pillow and was still.

And if that wasn't enough, *dayenu*, then Evie decided it was my turn. And when she put her hands on me, when she put her mouth on me, when she set my body on fire, I melted into the bed, *takeh*, like a puddle of *schmaltz* I was, all ooze and no bone. And then, hours later, when the moon had moved halfway across the sky and the stars were almost gone, we fell asleep, close, Evie's sweet little hand in mine.

The next morning we got up late, so quiet the house was, I knew it was empty except for that devilish look in Evie's eye. We picked up where we left off the night before, and so caught up in each other we was, we didn't hear my mother's foot on the step, we didn't hear her hand on the knob, my poor mother, so innocent she was, what did she know, she threw open the door and said, "So, *nu, Babka* Sisters, it's almost noon, ain't you getting up?" But of course we was up already, Evie was up on top of me, in fact, stark naked she was, her hips going up and down like a horse on a merry-go-round, her arms reaching for the sky.

"*Gottinyu, vey iss mir,* my God!" my mother shrieked.

Evie rushed to cover herself, the door slammed, I started to cry.

"Don't," Evie whispered, licking my tears like a puppy. "It's all my fault, I couldn't stop myself."

"What'll we do?" I wailed, but before Evie could answer, my mother came upstairs again. This time she knew enough to knock. "Ruthie, I think your friend better go home now," she said, my friend, she couldn't even say her name, and then one-two-three, Evie was gone.

Oy, was I in trouble, was my goose cooked, I'm telling you. My mother wouldn't even look on me, so ashamed she was. My father didn't know what to do, he knew something was wrong, but he didn't know what, my mother wouldn't speak of such things to him, but with one look she told him and my brothers I was in trouble but good. So no one talked to me at home, but never mind, I had bigger problems to worry about. On Monday when I went back to school, Evie was absent. I couldn't remember her ever being absent before and I was worried sick. What happened to her, did she hurt herself, did her parents know, too, were they punishing her, did she maybe run away? I only wanted to run to her house but I didn't dare, so much trouble I was in already, if I didn't come home right from school, my mother would kill me for sure. And I wanted to be right by the phone when Evie called, surely she would at least call? But call she didn't; instead a letter came. All typed up it was, all formal, like a business letter it was, *nu*, and this is what it said:

"Dear Ruthie:

I don't want to see you anymore. What we did was wrong, we should be ashamed of ourselves. It's a blessing your mother came in when she did; we're still young, we still have a chance to live the life God wants us to, with a husband and children and grandchildren, God willing. I am getting help from the rabbi, and I hope you will do the same." And she signed it "Evie," and that was all.

Turn off the tape recorder, will you, darling? I need a minute to catch my breath here, maybe a drink of water you could get me, there's a cup there, over by the sink. It still feels like a punch in the stomach, I remember reading that letter over and over, a thousand times I read it and all the while I could barely breathe. I called her of course, right away I called her, but her mother wouldn't let her come to the phone. She never even came back to school again, a few months later the whole family moved away, and Evie, my sweet, sweet Evie was gone.

So the years went by, life went on, it don't wait for nobody. I graduated from school, I got married, two children I had, a boy and a girl, I never really had feelings for my husband, but he was a good man, kind, a good provider, and my children, may they live and be well and call me once in a while, my children I loved of course, after all they are my own flesh and blood. With my husband, I did my duty, when he wanted me to come to him, I came, he deserved that much after all, and I tried not to let him know for me it was nothing, a waste of my time, but *nu*, such a thing is hard to hide, I think, *takeh*, he knew. I tried not to think about Evie, too painful it was, like a thousand knives going right through my heart, but every once in a while I couldn't help myself, I'd see someone who looked like her on the street and I'd wonder, where is she now, is she married, is she happy, is she all right, but of course I never knew.

And then one day, years later it was, the children were already married, I think my little granddaughter was already born, my little Madeline—ooh, you should have seen her, darling, so smart, so cute, like a little pumpernickel she was—anyway, one day out of nowhere, Evie's face came to me like a dream, like a vision, I just couldn't get her out of my mind. By this time my husband was gone already, he died young, a heart attack it was, did he love to eat, my Harry, I always told him to lighten up on the butter, go easy on the eggs, but did he listen to me? No, so *nu*, here I was, a widow at fifty-three, that ain't so old, but already I was going a little crazy, every time I turned around, Evie's face I saw, on the bus, on the TV, late at night when I closed my eyes. Five days it's like this and then all of a sudden, as sudden as she came, just as sudden, she's gone. And then four days after that, a letter I got, it fell into my hands from nowhere, straight out of the sky.

"Dear Ruthie," it said, "maybe you don't remember me, so many years it's been, and who knows, maybe it's best to let sleeping dogs lie. But I was in the hospital last week, five days I was there, a stroke they thought I had, an aneurysm maybe, they're still not sure, but I'm telling you, I almost died. A person changes from an experience like that, you know, I got home, everything looked different, I started thinking long and hard about my life, such a close call it was, but God in his wisdom took pity on me and gave me a second chance, don't ask me why. So *nu*, I started thinking about you, Ruthie, and I know you never wanted to see me again, you said so in the letter, I still have it, after all these years I could never throw it away, and maybe you still don't want to know from me, but I thought what could it hurt, so much time has passed, I'm going to write to you, and maybe you could write back to me and let me know you're still alive. Are you okay, Ruthie? Are you happy? Have you had a good life? If you don't want to answer, I'll understand, but I want you to know I never forgot you, and I ain't mad on you for what happened. Your old friend, Evie."

My heart started pounding so, I was only afraid I shouldn't have a heart attack, I sat down on the kitchen chair and read the letter again, once I read it, twice, a thousand times. I couldn't believe Evie had found me again after all these years. *Nu*, I'm still in the old neighborhood, I only moved a few blocks away, but still, I had a different last name, maybe she hired a detective, I didn't know, I was too excited, I only found out later she knew someone who knew someone who knew someone....you know it was a miracle from God that brought us back together, plain and simple, that's what it was. And finally after all these years, I knew what had happened, I put two and two together, I realized my mother wrote Evie a letter, the same letter Evie's mother wrote to me, and neither one could be further from the truth. I told Evie so, I sat down right then and there and wrote her a letter, my hand trembling so, I didn't know if she would be able to make out the words, so shaky they were on the page. I told her I loved her then and I loved her now, I told her how I couldn't stop thinking about her the five days she was in the hospital, like a vision she was, her face pale as a ghost. Two days later I picked up the phone and heard her voice, three days after that I picked her up at the airport and held her in my arms.

This time there was no one to hide from, no one to come up the stairs and disturb us, now we had all the time in the world to frolic in each other's arms. For days we stayed in bed, days and days and days, until I said, "Evie, *mamela*, we have to eat," and we stopped what we was doing to order in Chinese food and then got back in bed to feed each other with chopsticks, with our fingers, licking chow mein off each other, laughing all the time. At first I was shy with Evie, a blushing bride I wasn't no more, the flesh and the ground was having a meeting, you know what I'm saying, I wasn't no spring chicken, but Evie told me *shah.*

"You're beautiful, Ruthie, just like I remembered." And I remembered, too. My hand remembered her breast, my mouth remembered her thigh. Two widows we were, two grown-up ladies with grown-up children yet, it's hard for you to imagine, but oh, such a time we had, Evie and me, such noises that came out from our throats, our bodies bucking up and down so, I was only afraid we wouldn't break the bed and they'd find us there all in a tangle, two old ladies who couldn't *utz* themselves up from the floor.

You, you're young yet, you think you know from sex, but just wait, and boy did I wait, for over thirty years I waited to put my hands on her, my Evie, to lick her breasts, her belly, to drown once more in her smile, her eyes. Did we rock, did we roll, did we shriek, I'm surprised the house we didn't burn down, so hot for each other we were. It's a well-kept secret darling, but you should know, old ladies do know from such pleasures, believe me, you'll see, you think you got it good now, just you wait, you know, like they say, the best is yet to come.

I don't even regret the years we spent apart, Evie and I, God has his reasons after all, and I'm not even mad no more on my mother, may she rest in peace, she only did what she thought was best, she and Evie's mother, too. Evie and I had fourteen good years together until God looked down one day and said why should Ruthie Epstein have it so good, such a gorgeous *maideleh* she has, it's enough already, and God put up his hand and said to Evie, come, and so she did, so sweet she was, so good, God took a look and decided He wanted her all for Himself. All right, Evie and me, we've been separated before, God wants me down here and her up there, *nu,* who am I to complain, fourteen years we had, and boy did we make up for lost time, believe me, I'm telling you.

So that's all there is, there ain't no more, you can turn off your robot there, I told you enough, a secret I keep close to my heart that I never told nobody before, even my own children didn't know, why should I tell them? They thought it was so nice, a roommate I had, I shouldn't be so lonely, and when they came to visit, Evie slept in another bedroom, the house was big, we had plenty room. I'll tell you something, even when the children wasn't visiting, sometimes she slept in another room, when you're old sometimes you want to spread out, you got a little gas maybe, you need a night to yourself.

All right, I'm tired now, so much talking, talking, talking, but I hope you got what you wanted, I hope you get an A in your women's history class—all right, history, herstory, whatever, this is my story, it's a mystery, *nu*, why I was so lucky, so blessed, you should only be so lucky, may God shine such good fortune down on you. Believe me, God has his ways, *nu*, you think it's a coincidence that out of all the old ladies in this joint here, you picked me to interview, you came into my room? You and me, we've got something in common, we're cut from the same cloth, darling, *nu*, I can tell, and listen, *mamela*, it's nothing to be ashamed of, maybe your mother don't like it, your father, whoever, give them time, it's a different world today, they'll come around. You're young, you're a beautiful girl even with the purple eyebrows, *nu*, you should only live and be well and find your own Evie, God willing, and may she live and be well and have a long, happy life together with you.

Bagels and Bialeys

Gayle Brandeis

It all started when Toby Horwitz confessed to his wife that once, as a teenager, he had jacked off using a bagel.

"You did not!" Rachel tried to sound indignant, but she couldn't stop laughing, her black, curly hair spilling into her eyes. She shook her head and picked up an Everything from the platter that sat between them on the table, piled with bagels and bialeys from a deli on Fairfax. She turned it slowly around in her hand to inspect its sexual potential.

"Wasn't the hole a bit *big?*" she put her hand through the bagel so it dangled around her wrist like a bracelet.

"What? Are you disparaging my manhood?" Toby smacked Rachel playfully with a rolled up Calendar section from the *Los Angeles Times*. "You don't think I could fill up a bagel hole?"

"No, really," Rachel shook the bagel back onto her plate. Poppy and sesame seeds still clung to her arm, along with a few oily brown shreds of onion. "You know I think your manhood is lovely. But bagel holes are a bit—*roomy*, I guess you'd say? These are, at least. Then there are some you can't even stick your pinky through."

"The holes in the Sam Deli bagels were just the perfect size, honey," Toby stuck his tongue out at Rachel through a cranberry bagel and waggled it around.

"Wasn't it kind of *rough*?" Rachel was in her inquisitor mode, leaning back in her chair, arms folded over her chest.

"I slathered the inside of the hole with cream cheese," he grinned.

Rachel cocked an eyebrow.

"The ingenuity of the young and horny." Toby shrugged and dipped his finger into the whipped low-fat sun-dried tomato pesto cream cheese they both loved, and slid it into Rachel's mouth. She sucked it off distractedly.

"Don't tell me you've never looked at a bialey that way," said Toby, as if all women lusted after bread products.

Rachel shook her head with conviction, Toby's finger still in her mouth. She didn't tell him that she herself as a teenager had once committed a minor indiscretion with a kosher dill, a new one, still firm and bright green. The thought that a rabbi had blessed the jar made Rachel feel incredibly dirty afterward. She had difficulty looking at Rabbi Tepper for weeks.

Toby pulled his wet finger back and picked up a bagel and a bialey, one in each hand. "They're a perfect yoni and lingam, don't you think, Rache?"

"You know, I doubt they were designed with Indian mythology in mind," Rachel smiled. They had first met in a Hindu Art class at UCLA twelve years ago, a class that for some reason was teeming with Jews like themselves. The first time Toby asked Rachel out was the day they had learned about those anatomically suggestive stone fertility symbols. "You're only after my yoni, aren't you?" Rachel had replied sarcastically, but nevertheless, she had agreed to meet him for dinner that night at the kosher Indian restaurant, Bombay Bubbe's. She had been more than a little bit curious about his lingam, herself. Twelve years later, she was still curious, for which she was grateful.

"You never know." Toby now leaned across the table toward her, slowly bringing the bialey close to the bagel, sliding it through the lip of the hole, then drawing it back out again. "Things are often a lot more connected than they seem."

He started to move the bialey in and out of the bagel, slowly at first, but then faster and faster, until crumbs and seeds and hard garlic pellets were flying all over the place. Finally, Toby and Rachel had no other choice. What could they do but knock aside all the bread products and coffee and orange juice and newspapers? What could they do but make crazy, leavened love right there on the kitchen table, their bodies fitting together as perfectly as any stick and any hole—warm, wet flesh, or bread, or stone.

L'Chaim:
A *Shiksa's* Story

Carol Queen

I grew up in a house that looked across a valley, a wall of trees reaching up high as the sky, a river running down below. She grew up with canyons made of tall buildings, New York City rising all around. But she wound up on my side of the world, out West to go to school, and after the glass and concrete and brownstone she wanted to see the woods and the ocean. So we drove all over the back roads, up and down hills, looking at the land that was missing from her world—which until recently had looked like that famous *NewYorker* cover with New York's familiar streets stretching away, and tiny San Francisco an afterthought in the background. We *did* go to San Francisco together, but mostly we drove the back roads, pointing out deer and herons to each other, pulling over at scenic lookouts to read the little bronze plaques and learn the place's history. When the sunset was especially good we pulled over to fuck.

She dated only *shiksas* then, had as much of a fascination with the blonde, the WASP, or the Scandinavian surname as she did with the wild country settled by Okies. I grew up in the hills we traveled on our weekend road trips, in a town where the most ethnic it ever got was one Basque family (besides, of course, the displaced Indians living sullenly on the outskirts). That I grew up on a dirt road with a dad who raised sheep was a revelation to her; that she grew up wearing white lipstick, the leader of a gang of savvy Brooklyn girls, was more than a revelation to me. When she took me to New York I stared up at the buildings with awe, the hickest of *shiksas*.

"Come *on*," she'd say impatiently, pulling me back into the subway for another trip to see another wonder. When we got out it would be the Brooklyn Bridge or the Carnegie Deli.

When her mother met me she said I had nice skin.

I wondered about it, her dating only *shiksas*. But she grew up with practically nothing but Jews around her, her old grandparents and their peers, who had never really assimilated, still living so close to Ellis Island, where the immigration man couldn't spell their last names and simply shortened them. The ghosts of the Lower East Side, so close. It was romantic to me, but not to her. So she fucked *shiksas*, who appreciated her difference but didn't know too much about it.

I certainly appreciated it. My other, pale girlfriends turned transparent and vanished in comparison to her; she was lusty and intense, acerbic and funny, she had more personality than I had ever seen packed into one small person, and I adored her.

Until I met her, I had never met anyone who was not afraid of sex. Sex was so much her element that it made everyone else seem disconnected. I wanted to feel that comfortable, that at home in my body, that natural and adventuresome—and eventually I did.

To her it was awesome that I would pack a cooler and get in my van and drive up a mountain, find a place to camp and just sleep there, outside. To me it was awesome that she could masturbate and read the paper at the same time—I always had to concentrate when I did it, while for her it could be as desultory as scratching. She had once counted how many times she could come in one day, and I lost count at fifty-four. So when we made love, because I could come only perhaps twice, once in the morning and once at night, I would have to pace myself against her amazing capacity. But if I came too soon (and, unlike with men, that meant any time before forty-five minutes) she could keep going as long as she wanted by rubbing her clit—her lively, tireless clit—on my thigh or mons. I marveled that coming could be someone's forte this way, marveled when she came just by making me come. To be this orgasmic, I thought, she must have had an unbelievable head start—and it was true: she had been orgasmic since she was a little girl, and her mother had simply whispered to her that she ought to go into her own room for that. I don't remember what my mother said to me, but whatever it was, it worked: I didn't try it again till I was fifteen.

She loved to cook, and fixed me wonderful meals, murmuring, "Eat, *mamele*," just like her mother and grandmother had said to her. Though this was the 1970s and no one we knew possessed a dildo (or would admit to it), her well-stocked kitchen always contained something to play with if we got tired of fingers—and anyway, "Eat, *mamele*" could be taken two ways, if you thought about it.

Right before Christmas, with irritating *goyische* stuff in every shop and public building, we found ourselves in the grocery store looking twice at Santa's thick, cello-wrapped candy canes, nearly as big around as my wrist.

"Are you thinking what I'm thinking?" I asked, and we rushed home to celebrate the season with the most thrillingly naughty dildo imaginable. I hope that helped make up for all the annoying Christmases before and since.

We agreed as we combed the back roads that the West seemed to have no Jews, except recent immigrants like herself. The road trips took us into enemy territory on a regular basis. Shopkeepers at filling stations, the only businesses in towns off the interstate, would look at her suspiciously; she always got nervous when they said, "You're from New York City, arntcha?" She insisted this was code for "You're a Jew, huh?" A naive *shiksa*, I wasn't sure the hicks I grew up with knew a Jew when they saw one, or how they could connect her with the Trilateral Commission and the international banking conspiracy just by looking—but xenophobic about New Yorkers? You bet.

Still, her concern rubbed off on me, wise as I was in the way of small-minded country people. For that matter, Mr. and Mrs. John Birch Society wouldn't think much of the fact that we put our faces between each other's legs every chance we got. But nothing ever happened to us as we roamed through the small towns where people were trapped in small and bigoted lives.

On a trip to Portland I took her to an old and ostentatious deli, which, miraculously enough, she called a find, and after lunch we took a walk, stumbling on a beautiful old synagogue that had been built in the 1860s. If there were no Jews out here, who had built it? We slipped inside and read the plaques that detailed its history, learning together about the diaspora of German Jews that predated the one that brought her great-grandparents here from Russia.

We stayed up all night after we saw *Reds,* alternately talking and fucking, realizing we had predecessors. I idolized Emma Goldman. I told her about the young Jewish sisters who'd hosted Goldman when she traveled to San Francisco. Fifteen and sixteen years old, they'd headed an anarchist cell and recruited members from their synagogue. We talked about free love, though it was easier to talk about than to get right in the jealousy-plagued real world.

We talked all the time, about everything. She was passionate and opinionated. I was passionate and questioned everything. We stopped talking only when, locked in a savory, wet sixty-nine, we couldn't talk any more because our lips and tongues were too busy tracing every juicy inch of each other.

I took her to Crater Lake, crawled the van slowly up the mountainside, the elevation rising and the forest getting more and more sparse as we climbed. Up into the snow line my hand snaked into her overalls, found her pussy wet for me—if she could masturbate reading the paper, she could certainly enjoy the view while I drove one-handed. It was so early in the season that no one was there—the road had just been cleared—and the van putt-putted up the ridge in second gear. In my fingertips I felt her getting close, and I slowed, just a little.

"Wait, wait a second!" I swung around the last curve. The van topped the ridge. Out in the wide-open West, a wonder greater than New York ranged out before us: her first sight of Crater Lake, unearthly blue in its vast caldera, ringed by snowy mountains. Her thighs closed tight around my hand as she came hard, came loud, at the sight.

Now whenever I raise a toast, I don't say "Cheers!" What a noncommittal Brit saying. I say *"L'chaim!"*—to

51

life—always a little bit in her honor, because she taught me to taste life fully. *L'chaim*, my love.

By the way, she lives with a nice Jewish girl now, and I can come fifty-four times in one day.

Catholic Boys

Harvest Garfinkel

Nancy thoughtfully chewed her salad, wishing it had blue cheese dressing on it instead of whatever flavorless low-fat substitute she had ordered.

"I just can't help it. It's Catholic boys. Always has been. I just love 'em," she said.

"Well I think you're nuts," Diana shot back. "I know all about them. Catholic boys in the neighborhood. Catholic boys at school. Catholic boys at the store. Catholic boys on every goddamn corner. They're either afraid of women or contemptuous of us. And they can't fuck. Well, okay, except maybe the Italian ones. But they're all screwed up about sex in one way or another. You're Jewish. What's wrong with Jewish guys? I'm crazy about them. All that nice, soft, dark fur—they're definitely more sensual."

"I guess you should know, but I'm not feeling analytical right now. I just remember the Catholic boys I used to stare at on the bus in high school. You saw them only on the bus, 'cause they all went to parochial school. 'Bishop this or that' on their T-shirts. They had muscles and hard stares,"

Nancy said dreamily. "And they were different. You could never know them. There just wasn't any way. They didn't live in the neighborhood. And if they were at school they were never in my classes, 'cause you know, they majored in cars or something. Like there was this one guy in my study hall one year before I got out of going to them. Tom, his name was Tom. Jewish boys are never named Tom. And he was Polish, too. Not even Irish or Italian. Blonde hair and blue eyes, of course. Had to be blonde. And if he was in public school he had to be either really poor, or a very bad boy. He seemed like a bad boy. I felt outrageous just for checking him out. I guess I must have stared at him a lot, 'cause he changed his seat."

"Sounds more like a class thing than about Catholic boys," Diana said.

"Maybe," Nancy conceded. "But then again, look at the case of Dr. Sean Donavon. You couldn't call him working-class."

"A prick is what I'd call *him*," Diana retorted.

"He had one of those little gold crosses," Nancy sighed. "I love those."

"You, girl, are seriously deranged. I think maybe it's from lack of sex."

"Yeah, I love my job, but you just don't meet men being a gynecologist," Nancy replied as they left the restaurant.

In the taxi on the way to her office a succession of varied Catholic males ruled her daydreams. *Oh, Tom,* she thought, *Where are you now? Not in my office, that's for sure.* There waited only stacks of patients' charts and piles of horrid insurance forms, calling her just as surely now as her teenage longings had before.

She realized she had lost track of time when she heard

the housekeeping cart clatter down the hall. That certainly meant it was time for her to go home. She was plumped with satisfaction at the amount of paperwork she had slogged through. She was hungry again, the salad she'd eaten at dinner not even a memory to her stomach. Visions of veggie burgers dripping with melted cheese dotted her mind, and she unconsciously licked her mouth. Then she thought about her thighs. Okay, no cheese.

Her body felt stiff and cramped, and she got up to stretch. She was an ample woman, tall with large breasts, butt, and thighs. But she took care of her body because when she hit forty it had started complaining quite loudly if she didn't.

She was bent over, her thick, curly hair grazing the floor and her arms up behind her, when he came in. They were both startled; she straightened up so quickly she almost hurt her back.

Holy shit, she thought reverently, *this is the house-keeper?* They were supposed to be chubby ladies who muttered to themselves in obscure languages as they stolidly pushed mops and brooms. Another stereotype shot to hell. Because the person with the mop was nothing like that. The person with the mop was a young man and he was beautiful, booted, and blonde, with colorful stains on his black jeans. *Oy*, she thought, *an artist*. Her number-two weakness. She could not prevent herself from exploring every visible inch of him.

The fine hair on his arms was as fair as that on his head. A real blonde. And on his T-shirt she could just make out, in extremely faded lettering, "St. Ignatius Athletic Department." Unbelievable. Her eyes crept slowly up to his neck, and there it was: the tiniest gold cross on a very short chain. Wide, sharp cheekbones, wide, sharp mouth, pale blue eyes.

"Sorry. Didn't mean to surprise you. I do this office now; it's always been empty. Should I come back later?" His voice was devoid of inflection. *I hope this bitch isn't going to take too long,* he thought. *I want to go home.*

Nancy tried to regain her composure. She thought surely he must have noticed her lewd assessment of him; she had never been very subtle. She realized that she wanted him to notice and could feel herself flushing.

"No, I'm just finishing up here." *Please don't go away yet.*

"I'll go ahead and start then, if it's okay with you." He didn't pay much attention to what was in the places he cleaned, but he knew these were doctors' offices. *Shit,* he realized, *she's the pussy doctor.* He almost laughed. Why was she still standing there?

She saw the very dazzling dragon that stalked its way up his left arm. "Your dragon is really beautiful," she burst out, meaning it, but feeling stupid as soon as it was out of her mouth. Still, her body took a step forward; she felt an intense inner hollowness and was ruled by the need to have it filled.

"Thank you. I designed it," he offered.

He lifted out of his boredom enough to pay attention to her. There was a ripeness about her. She was older, past forty probably, but that wasn't it. She was rounded where he was used to planes. It was oddly attractive. He usually had sex with people who looked pretty much like himself, something he was conscious of but had no desire to examine. He had a sudden picture of burying himself completely in her flesh. Not just her cunt, but her whole body. There was some kind of ripe female smell. She was too far away for it to be coming from her. It must be coming from his mind.

Crap, he is a fucking artist, she thought. Or at least he

was at one time. The tattoo was exceptional. "Uh, didn't it hurt a lot?" *Oh, clever, Nancy.* She was starting to sweat. *Are we going back to high school here?*

He didn't answer, just smiled with one side of his mouth.

Then that other part of her took over, that part that went from the cunt up, instead of the head down. She backed up so she could sit on the edge of her desk. She swung one of her legs lightly. "Did you like it when it hurt? Just curious."

He laughed. "What?" *Was she coming on to him? Dr. Pussy and the janitor.* He could swear that smell was getting stronger.

"You heard me."

"Don't you think that's kind of an intimate question?"

She took a deep breath. "You decide," she said calmly.

"Part of me liked it and part of me didn't. I like to endure, you know?" She didn't seem put off by his answer, but he wondered if she knew what he was talking about.

Oh, goodie, she thought, briefly picturing him tied to a bed. So perfect for a Catholic boy, absolves him for whatever happens. She was getting wet. *God, hope I don't start squirming.* She took another deep breath and looked straight into his pale eyes.

What am I going to do with her? he wondered. He had no doubt she wanted him. He had always been able to tell when someone wanted him; even before he had the words to explain it, he felt it. Priests, his mother's friends, sometimes a friend of his father's. He could tell even when they didn't know it themselves. That look, that accidental touch that lingered—oh, he could tell. It didn't require a lot of insight to see what this one wanted. Yet he felt something absolutely innocent about her desire, almost as if she were a young girl. He hadn't been with anyone in several months, a long time for him. He had already had everyone he knew: female, male and in-between. Incredibly, he seemed to be growing tired of sex. Safe sex. A contradiction in terms.

Condoms, okay. Condoms by the box, always in their place on the floor next to the mattress. He had been lucky, really, that he had used them when he was very young, too, before anyone knew how you got that disease. You had to have one then, even if you had no hope of using it, just to piss off the Brothers if they found it. Even if he got a beating it was worth it just to piss them off. Besides, he wasn't about to have to marry some little rosary-bead-counting hypocrite just because of a moment's carelessness. He had tried to stay away from Catholic girls anyway. Jewish girls had been the best: the easiest to lay, and it wasn't serious for them, either. It was hard to get to them, though.

"So what's your name, anyway?" she asked. When in doubt, stick to the familiar.

"Tom, what's yours?"

"Tom? Your name is Tom?" she squeaked.

"Yeah, is that weird or something? It's a pretty common name."

Not where I come from, baby. "It's just, uh, one of my favorite names."

Strange. "I guess you're Nancy, huh? Dr. Nancy Kaplan," he said, reading her diploma. No wonder he'd been thinking about Jewish girls. "How do you do?" He grinned at his conscious use of the formal language, the first smile she'd seen. He was so damn cute. He offered her his hand to shake, part of the formality; he didn't know why he felt like being silly. He very seldom got silly. When she took the hand she refused to let it go. It was warm and dry and a little calloused. Hers was damp, but he didn't seem to mind. *Please kiss me.*

He drew her to him as though he had heard her thoughts and touched his lips to hers, just barely. Then he let his tongue out to lick her lips. Her mouth was much bigger than his, plump like the rest of her. He envied her those lips, never liking the thin mouth he saw in the mirror. But his tongue, well, he never worried about that. It had never disappointed him.

He ventured a little farther, just putting his tongue in and stroking hers softly. He always tried to tell what kind of kissing they liked. He figured he'd mastered all the available styles, and anything that involved his mouth made him happy. He quite liked the way she kissed back, though. He moved in close and held her all the way against him. He wanted her to feel his cock grow.

She was amazed that his skinny mouth was able to consume her. She was totally in cunt mode now; anyone who got her this far by kissing could have whatever he wanted. She offered a quick blessing to her Goddess, hoping he'd want something. Hoping he'd want a lot.

She broke for air and to look at him, and of its own accord her hand went up to smooth the hair back off his forehead. She quickly withdrew it, afraid it had been too intimate a gesture, but he smiled and did the same to her thick curls. He allowed his hands to linger there, twisting small ringlets.

"I like your hair," he said quietly.

"I like you," she returned, made bold by the steadily rising heat. She wanted to just put him in her pocket. "Come home with me?" Had she said that? It was out of her mouth without a thought. She really didn't do this sort of thing. Really.

Suddenly there was something unnerving about the situation. He didn't do this sort of thing anymore. He withdrew a little, and apparently she felt it, because she looked disappointed. Everything about this woman felt like warmth and kindness, and she was very sexy. Still, he sensed that there might be something more than a simple fuck going on here. He felt exposed in a way that he rarely did with anyone. Clearly his cock had no problem. It was up and waving frantically for his attention. It wasn't as though she were asking for a lifetime commitment. Probably she had a really nice house, too. She reminded him in some ways of those girls he'd wanted in high school. What the hell, he'd never had a doctor.

He took back her hand. "Sorry. I just haven't been with anyone for a while." It was a lame apology, he knew, but it would get them back where they wanted to be.

He didn't look to her like someone who went a long time between sexual encounters. But maybe she was making unfair assumptions because of his youth and aesthetic.

"So do you want to come home with me?"

He was still holding her hand, and he put it to his mouth and kissed her palm. "Sure."

"Where are we going?" he asked, wondering how long it would take for him to get home in the morning. He was surprised when she named a part of the city that was relatively inexpensive.

She laughed. "Thought I was rich, huh? Rich doctor fantasies? Sorry to disappoint you. I don't have that kind of practice. I've always treated a percentage of women who don't have insurance. You don't get rich that way. And I don't own the house, I rent, and it's a flat, and I'm not good with money, okay?"

"Yeah, I was kind of hoping for something a little more glamorous. I have friends who live around there."

"Well, at least it's just a short train ride away," she said cheerfully.

"Excuse me, you don't have a car either?"

She was laughing now. "I have one. I just don't take it to work. Who drives a car downtown? The traffic's crazy."

He was beginning to regret this again. He was tired after working. He hoped they wouldn't have to walk far from the train to her house. He needed a shower, too; he could smell himself. But she put her arms around him in the elevator and kissed him so sweetly he couldn't refuse her.

"I'll feel you up on the train," she said with a small giggle.

And she did, too. She made him take the inside seat, and she sat sideways, facing him. She put her hand between his legs and caressed his cock through his jeans until she felt it begin to move. Then she switched her hand around to the back and inserted it into that little gap between his shirt and the top of his pants. Oh, he was wearing underwear. She got almost giddy with lust at the thought of him in his little cotton panties.

The situation made him a bit nervous. Not than he hadn't engaged in his share of outrageous behavior. But he had expected something a bit more conventional from her. Maybe he even wanted that. Milk and cookies. An image of his mother passed unwanted through his mind. *Oh, please. Think about that later.* Her hand continued to move and his jeans felt too tight. All right, she was full of contradictions, but he had to admit that was part of her attraction. Like he had loved the way she was wearing a big, sloppy men's style cardigan sweater over a lace top. Probably one of those body suits that were so hard to take off.

He leaned over and pulled her top down over her bra, then reached inside and held a breast. He heard her gasp, and the nipple hardened as he pinched it lightly. It felt quite large. He imagined his mouth around it. He smiled against her neck. Milk and cookies. She was moving her pelvis slightly on his hip—but then she pulled back. By then they had provided fantasy material for several of their fellow passengers.

Nancy settled back in her seat.

"So, when was the last time you went to confession?" she asked, striving for a neutral tone.

"What?" he sputtered, thinking, *Shit, I've still got a hard-on and she's asking me about sacraments? What is going on with this chick?* "What are you talking about?"

"Well, I was just wondering, here's a nice Polish boy with a cross around his neck, has to be Catholic, right? I'm wondering is he going to go say he's sorry tomorrow for what he does tonight?"

"Lady, I stopped believing in that crap when I was twelve."

"Then how come you're wearing that cross? Not that it doesn't look lovely," she hastened to add.

"It's an ironic gesture, a juxtaposition of opposites for artistic effect. Goes good with the dragon, don't you think?"

"Uh-huh. Who gave it to you?" she pushed, seemingly innocent as she relentlessly advanced on his psyche.

"It's 24-carat gold," he said weakly.

"Mother gave it to you, huh?"

The hell with this bitch. No mothers. Mothers are not happening. Churches are not happening. "Why are we having this conversation?" *Why am I still hard?*

He's angry. I stepped into something. She didn't want to admit she'd done it on purpose.

"I'm sorry, really sorry. I didn't mean to offend you." She took a deep breath. "I just sort of have a thing for Catholic boys. Or ex-Catholic now, I guess. It's a teenage fetish. I never got over it."

"I'm not some fucking symbol, you know."

"I know. I don't think you are. You're just very attractive." She was pleading effectively with her dark brown eyes.

He relented. "How'd you know I was Polish?"

"Just a good guess. Lots of 'em where I grew up. What's your last name anyway?"

"Pulaski," he said with resignation.

"Mmm, an aristocrat," she said, surprising him.

"Yeah, well everybody named Windsor isn't related to Queen Elizabeth, you know. Believe me, there weren't any castles where I grew up."

As they approached her house, an abrupt spasm of terror knifed its way through her gut. *Who is this guy? What the fuck are you doing? What if he's dangerous—he looks kind of dangerous.* Of course that was sexy. And it was mostly image, anyway... *I can't stop now, so I might as well trust him.* Besides, Tony and Emmett downstairs would hear if she screamed

He was holding her hand, and felt her tense up; he knew what she must be thinking. *Lady, if you only knew. I'm probably more scared than you.* She was too warm and too soft and he was afraid he'd sink in and never get out. God, he had to stop thinking about his mother.

Her place was interesting, if messy. Some of the art she

had was original, he knew, probably bought at a tiny gallery or even on the street from fools like him who couldn't give up that dream of making a living from their art. Every year he'd sell just enough to make him believe it could happen. From what he saw, she'd probably like his work. She'd go nuts if she ever saw the ones with the crosses. But he didn't show those to anybody.

"It's a nice place."

"Yeah. It's got a little yard in the back; I share it with the guys downstairs. We have a garden."

They went into the kitchen. It was big and comfortable and had windows. It looked like a place that got used. He could cook; somehow he had absorbed the knowledge from watching his mother when she was all alone and made him stay with her. He'd watch her and draw when he had the stuff to draw with.

"Want something to eat? I'm hungry. How about a nice sandwich or something?" She was half making fun of herself, but at the same time she knew she wanted to feed him almost as much as she wanted to fuck him.

He laughed out loud. Milk and cookies after all.

He came back after having taken a shower, clean and fed. She took his hand and led him to her bedroom. She stopped just short of the bed and kissed him, taking her time about it. He was feeling her whole mouth and letting her in to do the same, and each knew by intuition when to advance and withdraw. *Tongues talking*, she thought. Tom did love her mouth. After all, her kiss was probably what got him here in the first place.

Nancy pulled him onto the bed with their clothes still on, then opened a drawer one-handed and threw out a variety of gloves, condoms, lubes, and other paraphernalia. Tom unzipped her jeans, stopping to admire her round tummy with his palm before pulling them off. "You little slut, you're not wearing panties," he grinned. "I like that in a person." She responded by quickly stripping his bottom. He took his own shirt off, hoping she would get the hint and do that bodysuit: he couldn't understand how anyone got them on, let alone how to take one off someone else.

Tom had wanted to put her tits in his mouth since the train. She wrapped herself around him as she felt that electric line switch on, the one that went from her breast to her cunt. Everything he did with his mouth was so good. He put some lube on his fingers and stroked it on her pussy.

"Show me how you like it," he said, putting her hand down there. His head was between her legs so he could watch her. Precome was leaking profusely from his slit, and he was using it and the lube to play with himself.

It was exciting to watch him. He had a pretty cock. There were all kinds: cute ones, butch ones, sweet ones, even beckoning ones—but his—well, it was pretty. It was dark pink and resiliently hard at the moment. He hadn't been cut, another forbidden thrill for Nancy, and his foreskin was long so that there was a short turtleneck around the smooth head.

He started to use his tongue on her, teasing with light, quick motions. He rubbed his distended organ against the sheet and stuck his tongue all the way into her slit, wide open now. His face was covered with her; it was like drinking from a well. She was twisting around and he was surprised at her strength. She was fairly tall but not that big; he could feel the layer of muscle underneath the soft padding of her curves. She grabbed his head and shoved it harder into herself.

"Put your face in there. Use your nose." She locked her legs around him. They both knew he could break her hold if he chose, but he didn't. He did what she told him to do, and she relaxed. Soon she stiffened and bucked and yelled her orgasm.

He turned over on his back and plopped her down on top of himself. *Likes the bottom,* she noted hazily. *I was right. Sit on his face?* she wondered. Or how about those nipples, they were the same color as his dick. Nancy was crazy about that color, kind of dark for a blonde. She flicked them with her fingertips, lightly at first, then more roughly, using her fingernails too. They rewarded her by turning into hard points. She gave them a final twist as he groaned and thrust his hips back and forth, then indulged her fantasy, the ultimate Catholic-boy fantasy. She put his little gold cross in her mouth and sucked on it. He twisted away, startled, and she mocked, "Did that disturb you? I thought you just wore that for a joke, a little prank, right?"

He was a mix of out-of-control feelings, bewildered by the intensity of his desire for her. He had been right. There was more than a simple pick-up fuck here, if he wanted it. If she wanted it.

She reached down and picked up a glove and some lube. When he saw what she was doing, he slowly moved his knees apart and bent his legs, looking into her face the whole time. She licked around the head of his cock and applied some moderate pressure to his asshole, which was that same shade of dark pink. He was loose enough to allow her finger to slip in fairly easily. She moved it around shallowly and then added a second finger, going deeper, watching for signs that she'd hurt him. When he shoved himself back against her fingers, she searched for that gland to stroke. A scream confirmed that she had found it.

"If you keep doing that I'm gonna come," he hissed.

She stopped then, not because she didn't want him to come, but because she felt there was something just not right. She wanted to give this man something special. "This is all real easy for you, huh? You surrender very nicely. I imagine you've done it before."

He held his breath, not knowing where this was going. He had not expected this from her, and he didn't think he wanted it. But he also knew he wouldn't stop her.

Nancy was working on blind intuition. "Stand up for me."

Tom looked confused but did as she asked. She knelt in front of him with her long curls brushing the floor. "What do you want me to do?" she asked. "You own me. I'm here to serve you."

Nancy looked up so he could see that she was serious. She saw fear skitter across his face and the tension in his body. *You can do it, Tommy. Be in charge.*

He felt like crying. He realized he was frightened. Never had he been this scared when somebody else was in control. He looked down at her. She was licking his feet. Suddenly, joy ripped through him in all the places where the fear had been. He was possessed.

"You don't do anything unless I tell you to," he said.

"Yes," she whispered.

"You know better than that," he said calmly. "Yes, what?"

Okay, girl, if you're going to do this, you'd better do it. And don't laugh. "Yes, Sir."

He was half hard. "Suck me," he said in a louder voice. She raised her head to obey him, and he slowly fucked her mouth as he lengthened. He was all the way hard and his erection was pushing against the back of her throat. She gagged, and kept on sucking as hard as she could. She was drooling all over herself. She did belong to him, at least for this moment.

"That's enough." He spread his legs. "Lick my asshole. Make love to it." She grabbed the nearest piece of latex and scurried behind him to do as he said. Goddess, he did have a beautiful butt. Round globes that dimpled as she held them. She buried her face in the crack of his behind, and suddenly her boundaries disappeared. She was everywhere, supreme and yet annihilated. She filled the whole room, the whole house, the whole world, and yet she was nothing.

"Harder," he said. "I can't feel it through that shit. Put your tongue inside."

Erotic energy ran through him in a way he had never experienced before. *I deserve to feel this good*, he thought.

"Please my Lord, fuck me. Please," Nancy begged, meaning it.

"Back on your hands and knees," he told her, and she almost came when he said it. "Put the rubber on me. Do it nice." She did it with her mouth.

His cock went in from behind and she angled herself up, shamelessly trying to get it farther inside. He was fucking her hard, hitting against her G-spot, and slapping her butt while he did it. She couldn't tell how hard he was hitting her because it all felt so good. The sounds they made were impossibly arousing. When he came he yelled almost as loud as she did.

When they crawled back into the bed from their pile on the floor, cuddling together, Tom's face was luminous and he looked very beautiful.

"See, I said you were an aristocrat. You can be my

Prince. World, this is Prince Pulaski."

"Something happened to me," he said in wonder.

"It's just magic, baby. Go to sleep now."

Catholic boys. The fire of that unleashed sexuality was the more brilliant for having to work through guilt and repression.

Catholic boys. If they ever figured it out, they *really* figured it out.

Mother Was Right

Judith Arcana

I remember he had blonde hair so straight it wouldn't curl if you threatened it. Light eyes with maybe three or four yellow lashes on each eyelid. Beige eyebrows. He taught at a college called William of Orange. What kind of a name is that for a college? Only the *goyim!*

When he took off his underpants, I saw right away that his penis was too big. I don't mean too big for me; I'm a big girl. I mean too big for *him*. He was wearing somebody else's penis by mistake. I was used to the body of a Jewish bear, hairy, weighty, and thick, but this little *goy* was so light I could flip him over in bed, roll over and over holding him pressed against me. So that just couldn't be his penis. But there it was, hanging, and for a minute my vision blurred; I imagined it dangled to his knees.

Is this possible? Such a little nose and such a big *shlong?* Could anybody suck this elephant's trunk? And what about all that wrinkled skin? Do you just roll it up, like putting on panty hose? Or will it retract into his body, like his balls on a cold day? Could I even consider eating such *trayf?*

With his giant sausage, this uncut gentile goes into Jewish girls. His ex-wife is a Jew. And she's so tiny, that one. What did she do with it? It's so big, all you can do is store it, I guess. She must have always been looking for some place to put it. Well, he's found the place for his *goyishe putz*—he brings it to nice Jewish girls who wish only to oblige Prince Valiant, to let him unfurl his Christian banner at our gates.

Blinded by the passion that brought me to this greatest of all gifts, the love of a blondie, for a while I didn't even realize that my *goyishe* lover couldn't keep his erection. Actually, I just couldn't tell the difference; it lay there, a log across my thighs. Even soft, it seemed hard; the weight really fooled me.

But this can't be an ethnic trait, I thought. *Surely there are Garfinkels and Weissbergs with sticks like this.* Right away, in fact, I thought of the Stein kid. He'd been a student of mine when I was a high school teacher. Years after he graduated, I fucked him in a tiny wooden loft in a cabin in Santa Cruz. He had a huge penis, sort of thick, but length was the remarkable feature, like linguine. And his worked fine. The Stein kid had no trouble with erections; in fact, we almost had to break it to get rid of his erection.

So size is not the issue. It isn't true that when it gets that big, you just can't lift it. (Right, and there was that other young one, Rosenbloom, the artist. When he got it up, he didn't know where to put it, and he thought he wasn't allowed to use his hands. But I digress.)

No, it's not about size; maybe it's that chemise they wear. I'd never before seen one that wasn't circumcised. My husband's clean Jewish penis had been smooth and honest, no secrets. But these guys could be hiding anything—what have they got up that sleeve? Is this why we're not supposed to do it with them?

Maybe we've been taught to avoid them because you can't know what you're getting; there's no opportunity for a truth-in-packaging guarantee. They hide their heads, these *goyim*, they cover their tiny mouths with fleshy cheesecloth. Lack of boldness, is it? They're secretive about their desire? What are they afraid of?

Freud got it confused, all that *meshugeneh* business about women having penis envy—maybe the real problem in this Christian country is penis shame. Are they hiding, these blonde boys? Do they want to be coaxed out of their flaccid anxiety?

Like that other one, the pilot. He was even circumcised, I think. But he had the same problem; his *schmuck* was shy. Okay, so it's not the fact of being hidden, it's all in their minds? So my mother was warning me against disappointment all those years—she knew they were troubled, disturbed?

Yes, he was definitely circumcised, I remember now, and he even had kinky hair—yellow frizz, a novelty item. But sure enough, when we finally got naked together, he couldn't hold his head up. Now this wasn't love, like with William of Orange. This was lust and we both knew it. We flirted, teased, and talked about it constantly, and once I was sure he was as hot as I was, I took off work to spend a day in his apartment.

The irony is that while we were still in those early stages of mutual fascination, I heard all these stories about his prowess. Paeans to his talent were scrawled on the walls of women's toilets up and down Lincoln Avenue. The bars were full of women who'd done it with him—and gave referrals; the guy had an actual reputation.

I read one of those scrawls a couple of months afterward, in a stall at the old Oxford Pub. "Chuck Thompson is a great lay," a woman had printed above the sanitary napkin disposal box. No marking pen in my pockets, I could only vocalize my reply: "I beg to differ, honey; Chuck Thompson is no lay at all."

So what's the story? Are they all like that? I remember Karl—a German, may the *Shekhina* forgive my childish folly—in college in 1960. This was before I went all the way, so we were hot most of the time we were together. I was seventeen; he was twenty, but he was way behind my Jewish high school boyfriend. He actually ran into the bathroom to jerk off when our grinding on the couch in his apartment brought him near ejaculation. He panted, "Somethin's comin' in my pants," leaped off me, and dashed for the toilet.

I'd never known a Jew to do such a thing. I mean, of course he would come in his pants. Hopefully, so would I. That was the idea, right? Sticky jockey shorts were par for the course in our generation; didn't these Christian boys want to get it off?

Ricky Greenglass, my high school steady, had been a model lover for a fifteen-year-old-girl. He was kind of messy and a little foolish, but cute—and he could have been a sculptor, a pianist, with those fingers. He was good for hours; life-size statues he could have molded, whole symphonies he might have played in my teenage vulva, when my clitoris turned sweet sixteen.

Okay, in fairness, I have to say that there was that pale blonde pizza delivery boy who kissed with intense suction. He may have been the exceptional *shaygetz*, but we never got far enough for me to find out.

But what about it? When the professor could finally fuck, he turned out to be mainly interested in the piston effect: up and down, in and out. He could do it a long time, but I lost interest. And the pilot—what he wanted, as we turned to each other on his king-sized mattress in the morning sunlight, was the immediate grab. I was pretty excited, licking his throat, sliding my legs along his, when—after less than three minutes—he suddenly asked, with a slight gesture toward his groin, "Are you ignoring me?"

Ignoring him? I was practically enveloping him! I explained that I wasn't the early bird out after a worm, and that we literally had all day, so why didn't we just take our time? He mumbled, "Sure, sure," but he didn't mean it.

So. Were Jewish girls forbidden the *shaygetz* because our mothers knew that they wouldn't do right by us? Does their gear work right only when they do it with gentile girls? Or—incredible—does it never really work right? Has this recollection of youthful fumbling uncovered the reason so many of my Christian girlfriends' mothers urged them to find a Jewish husband? Is this what those *shiksas* wanted to know when they asked, "Is it true that they learn in Hebrew school to make girls happy?"

Did my mother know, in 1956, that the sexual frustration of women would become a major cultural issue before her daughter was thirty? Was she protecting me when on my thirteenth birthday she astonished me by saying, "No more gentile boys. You're too old now."?

I can hear them now, my mother and Anita in *West Side Story*—yes, it's Bella Solomon singing a duet with Rita Moreno, and they're both *shrying* at me: "One of your own kind! Stick to your own kind!" I seem to have come round again to that familiar point in my life when I blink, stretch my mouth into a comic O, and recognize a cosmic truth: for practical purposes, my mother was right.

Shayna's *Shabbat*

Claudine Taupin

*Yah! How I long for the bliss of the
Shabbat
united in secret with Your own fer
vent wish.
Give way to Your own deep desire to
love us.
May Sabbath in Torah be our
sacred bliss.
Share Her with us who desire to
please You —
Our deep thirst for union be met
with delight.*

*From a Sabbath hymn, "Yah Ekhsof
Noam Shabbat," by Reb Ahron of Karlin.*

The Sabbath, *shabbes*, the presence of the Queen on the
holy seventh day of the week. On this night more than any
other, I welcome in the presence of the *Shekhinah*, concep-

tually the feminine presence and manifestation of Ha-Shem, the ever-present spiritual force that represents the Oneness of all creations big and small.

In my life, Sabbath tradition takes precedence over perhaps all other forms of Jewish observance. In terms of utmost simplicity, it is a day of rest from secular activity, a period of reflection, spiritual focus, study, and sexual union. Friday afternoon brings with it a rush of pre-*shabbes* activity. I hurry to finish my work, then tidy my home office for Sunday, the next working day. I braid the dough into the shape of a *challah*, and smother the top with sesame seeds that soon fill my house with a delicious, sensual, oven-baked smell. With the dinner menu planned and the ingredients chosen, I hurry to shower and dress myself.

I turn on the shower, discard my work clothes—sweatpants, T-shirt, flannel, slippers—a mass of dark-colored clothing forms a puddle on the floor of my steam-filled bathroom. The water is near-scalding, a fiery temperature that brings the blood to the surface of my skin. Methodically and quickly, I wash my armpits, back, arms, face, neck, breasts, and legs. I part the lips of my vagina slightly and allow the hot water to trickle in and down my legs. I lather myself with a deliciously scented soap, rubbing my fingers in and over every crevice. I turn my back to the showerhead and lean forward to allow the water and soap to rinse my backside. Cleansed, I turn around again to shave my legs of the dark, short hair that covers them. The tattoos that grace my feet and lower legs come to life with vibrant color. I look down at my dark pussy hair, a wildly untamed and curly bush, and decide to shave it as well. Seconds later, my fold is covered by a narrower brush of hair; it is no less curly or dark, simply tamed to a sleeker version of its natural shape.

Out of the shower, I towel myself dry, standing before a wide mirror that reflects my earthly image to me. A medium-height, dark-haired, Semitic-featured woman looks back at me. There have always been things I have loved and disliked about this body. Lately, I've taken on a more athletic look; strong thighs, well-developed calves and biceps, and slightly visible stomach muscles. Ah, but there's that *zaftig* rear end. It never seems to diminish in size. My ancestors have given me such a *tuchus*—no amount of exercise ever reduces its bountiful proportions. My breasts bring me no particular sense of pride or accomplishment—they are average breasts, and they hang a bit lower than I would like. Their bounciness is a bother when I exercise, but I am always reminded of their worth when my husband buries his head in between them, or wraps his teeth around my red-brown nipples. A baby would like these breasts. *Nu*, who am I to complain?

I'm shivering—it's too cold in the house. I turn on the heaters and walk to my bedroom. There are no mirrors here. I've gotten used to dressing without mirrors—preferring to dress by feel and emotion rather than by image. Tonight, the feeling is soft, sensual, slightly wicked. I find a dark-colored, somewhat see-through bra that hoists my breasts up to form the kind of cleavage that nature, in her confusing benevolence, did not grant me. I slip into an older dress that still feels as seductively soft as when I first purchased it—a dark, forest green velvet gown with a tight bodice and near floor-length hem. Deftly, I wrap my hair up in an elaborate twist with the aid of a black scarf, adding a black velvet choker and a pair of polished silver hoop earrings. Underneath, I slip on a pair of black thong panties, knowing that my rear end looks inviting to my husband, Abram, this way. I forego tights or pantyhose—they're rarely worth the trouble it takes to put them on or, more important, to take them off.

Barefoot, I walk downstairs to the kitchen, stopping along the way to turn on an eclectic, local college radio station. A fast-paced funk song is coming to an end and the DJ introduces the next piece, an endearing klezmer piece that starts off with Yiddish exclamations I am only barely able to understand. The song gets going full swing—the perfect background accompaniment to my frenetic dinner preparations.

I reach for my apron, a worn hand-me-down that dates back two generations and has spanned a few thousand miles. The still elegant wraparound apron is dark blue, with vertical patterned flowers. My husband has always commented affectionately that I look like quite the Jewish *yenta* in my apron and with my hair up, concealed or framed by dark-colored scarves.

I pull out my worn cutting board and begin to chop carrots, onions, mushrooms, and potatoes. I throw together a *matzah* ball mix and leave it to chill in the refrigerator. I throw the vegetables and assorted herbs into boiling water and leave the entire mixture to simmer in a generously sized stock pot. I get to work on a vegetarian version of a shepherd's pie to accompany my soup, draining and pressing tofu, boiling more potatoes, stirring together a convincing nonmeat gravy that has become a coveted trade secret in my kitchen.

I glance outside and realize that the sun has just begun to set, and I hurriedly set up my *shabbes* candles on the dining-room table. I hear Abram's keys right outside the door—he's home just in time. Abram's handsome, olive-toned face greets me. Taking a quick whiff of the smell filling the living room, he beams an appreciative smile in the direction of the kitchen. "*Matzah* ball soup?" he asks. I nod and perform an amusing little curtsey.

"At your service, m'lord," I laugh.

Abram chuckles and puts down his bag. "You'd better be careful," he says. "I may just take you up on that."

After removing his shoes, Abram walks over, wraps a strong arm around my waist, and leans down to kiss me on the cheek. "*Gut shabbes*," he whispers.

"*Gut shabbes*," I reply. "Let's light the candles."

Abram lights the candles as I chant the traditional prayer and cover my eyes with the palms of my hands. Abram looks at me appreciatively, and I continue with the rest of the prayers. We each drink a small cup of *kiddush* wine, ceremonially wash our hands, and break the *challah*, which comes fresh from the oven.

"I've got to go finish the soup. Come with me and tell me about your day," I say.

Abram nods and follows me into the kitchen. He leans against the sink while I busy myself rolling *matzah* balls from the refrigerated mixture.

"I love that dress," he sighs. "You look so ravishing in it."

Such compliments melt my heart, and he knows it. I turn around to smile at him. Abram has folded his powerful arms across his chest. He's wearing a short-sleeved black shirt and adorably sexy black jeans.

"You look pretty good yourself, Abram. "

I turn my back and continue putting the rolled balls of *matzah* mixture into the soup. I'm somewhat startled to feel Abram's warm breath on my neck.

"Hey! What are you doing?! Stop bothering the chef, please," I protest.

Abram doesn't say anything in response. He presses his

body against my dress and reaches around to touch my breasts.

"Beautiful," he mumbles into my ear. "You're so beautiful, Shayna."

I reach down for the towel hanging from the oven door and wipe the remainder of the mixture from my hands.

"Abram...what are you doing?" I ask again, in a softer voice.

Abram's hand moves up from my breasts to my neck. He tugs at my choker, creating a slightly uncomfortable but enormously pleasant sensation. I lean back to expose my throat even more.

Abram strokes my throat, stopping to tug on the choker a few more times. The sensation is unbearably exciting. He presses the front of his jeans into my backside. Even through the fabric of my dress, I can feel his large, straining cock up against the crack of my buttocks. Abram groans softly. He undoes the tie of my apron and pulls it off.

I feel flushed and utterly turned on. "What's gotten into you, Abram?" I manage to say. "Are you about to make love to me right here on the kitchen floor?"

Abram pulls up my dress. "Have mercy," he laughs gently. "Look at this *tuchus* of yours. It's a dream come true."

With my back turned, I can't see Abram's expression, but I can sense his level of arousal.

"Bend over a little for me, Shayna," he urges. "Bend over and spread your legs just a little bit."

Next to oral sex and vigorous fucking, being spanked is my favorite form of sexual activity. Abram knows this, and he likes it. I comply with his request and lean forward over the stove, with my legs spread slightly. The *matzah* ball soup steams and bubbles close to me, filling my nostrils with a pleasant aroma.

A few seconds pass in complete silence. I know not to

turn around to look; the implicit rules of our sexual games state that he is allowed to do as he wishes with me when I assume a position like this. I hear him unbuttoning his jeans.

"Shayna, I've been fantasizing about this all day," he says in a voice tinged with excitement. "I couldn't wait to come home and look at my beautiful wife."

I can tell by the sound of it that Abram is stroking his cock. He groans softly again. I stay in my position, arching my back slightly so as to give him a better view of my ass and my shaved pussy, barely contained within the fabric of my black panties.

A sharp slap on my ass greets my movement. The pain is gone in an instant, but I'm left panting for more. Abram rewards my moans with three more quick slaps, and then he sinks to his knees. Now underneath my dress, his face moves forward to taste my honey. I bend my knees slightly to lower myself to a better position. Eagerly, he pushes aside my panties and begins to lick at my opening, making small, muffled noises of excitement, which I can barely hear through my own cries and moans. His hand comes up to play with my clit, causing me to shiver with pleasure.

Over the six years of our marriage, I've learned that Abram never does any one thing for too long. While I would be content sucking his beautifully circumcised cock all night long, Abram's theory of what works best to pleasure me is to keep stimulating me in various ways until I reach the point of orgasm.

Abram leaves one finger resting on my clit while his other hand teases the opening of my wet pussy. Two of his long, narrow fingers press upward, barely inserting themselves into my vagina. His hand rests this way for a short time while the finger on my clit rubs me in a slow, circular motion. I'm weak from the pleasure of it all, and I steady myself against the stove. Abram removes his hand from my clit and reaches back to squeeze my ass, then pulls away the fabric of my thong. One of his fingers gently brushes against my anus, just as he pushes his two strong fingers deeper inside my pussy. With mad passion, I fuck his fingers, sliding them deeper inside me.

Abram can clearly sense that I am on the verge of coming. He pulls his wet fingers out from inside me and emerges from underneath my dress. He turns me around, and we kiss fervently with our tongues, pressing our bodies close. I can taste the faint, commingling flavors of my juices and the soap with which I just cleansed myself.

"Abram," I plead, "make me come."

"Up against the wall," he demands playfully.

Again, I comply, although unsure about what Abram intends to do.

As I face him, with my back resting against the kitchen wall, Abram pulls off his jeans, grabs hold of my waist, and lifts me up off my feet. His straight, thick, dark cock pulses with anticipation. After years of looking at Abram's body, I am still awed by the beauty and perfection of his organ. Abram positions himself underneath me and brings me down toward him so that my opening is touching the tip of his cock.

I let out a sharp scream of delight as he lowers me down toward his body. His engorged cock fills me, and the sensation of dangling a few inches above the kitchen floor is enough to send me into waves of pre-orgasmic pleasure. I look down at Abram's straining, muscular body and at his face, which is set in an expression of sheer enjoyment and concentration. I reach down to rub my clit as Abram bucks against my body, his hands tightening against my waist.

As the force of his movement carries me to orgasm, I

throw my head back against the wall. My body shakes violently, and Abram struggles to hold me up as he shoots his warm come inside me. He groans loudly, uttering my name as he finishes emptying his load.

In one quick motion, Abram pulls out and sets me back down on the floor. He leans against me, breathless, and kisses me softly on my lips.

"Gut shabbes, Shayna," he laughs softly.

"I'll send you right to bed without dinner if you've ruined my soup," I reply while straightening my dress. "Just sit down at the table and behave yourself."

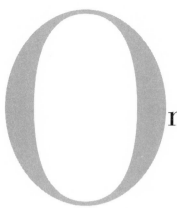ne Single Night

Susannah J. Herbert

Two days until the wedding! I was one of the last of my friends, male or female, to get married, and I was still incredulous that it was happening. That David wanted a *chuppah* had surprised me almost as much as the proposal that came after we'd been together for over seven years. I had been happy enough as we were, but we talked, and the next thing I knew we were registered for stemware.

It was Friday night. David, newfound piety notwithstanding, was about to spend his final *Erev Shabbat* as a single man at that last of all socially accepted bacchanals: his bachelor party.

I tried to be nonchalant about it, despite the fact that David's best friend, Phillip, was coordinating the evening, under the sort of security usually reserved for the joint chiefs of staff.

Let's be honest: as I watched David dress to go out, I felt threatened. Hard to admit, but true. Phillip was a great guy and I knew he liked me, but his libido ran somewhere between those of the Marquis de Sade and Howard Stern. I asked David what men did at "those things." Whores, strippers, what? This wasn't mere jealously; let's not forget it's the end of the millennium and sex isn't always safe.

He laughed and told me not to worry. (Did this mean he'd be chaste, or wear condoms when fucking the harem-for-hire?)

I teasingly reminded him it was *Shabbat,* the holiest of nights. He repeated what the rabbi had told us: it was a *mitzvah* to make love on the sabbath. We giggled, two Jews who went to *shul* once a year on the High Holy Days and saw nothing wrong with Christmas carols or crispy bacon. Eager to perform a *mitzvah* on this sacred occasion, I kissed my lover and ran my hand along his crotch. His familiar hard-on grew instantly in my hand. I dropped to my knees, unzipped his black cords, and sucked him. For once, foreplay held no interest for me. I wanted him hard and I wanted him now.

I grabbed his round, soft ass and took his cock into my throat. Backed against the bedroom wall, he caressed my hair and thrust into my mouth. He grabbed at my sweater so he could suck my breast while simultaneously working to pull off my pants. Had it not been so hot, his awkward enthusiasm would have been humorous. Usually a playful lover, today his actions were anything but carefree. He kissed me hotly, then in one fluid motion turned and dipped his tongue into my cunt.

We were on the floor, hungrily licking and sucking at each other's centers. Every move was deliberate, wild. He kissed my clit and penetrated my core with one, two, three fingers. I knew the spots that drove him wild, and I visited them with my tongue, my knuckle, the flat of my hand. As my cunt began to shake, contracting around his fingers, I turned to his ass and flicked my tongue across the dank, puckered darkness. He cried out and mirrored my actions with his tongue in my cunt. I moved my lips to his cock, using my wet fingers to tickle his balls and bum. With a primal moan, he bucked and exploded. I swallowed the warm cream and slowed my rhythm, reveling in each wild spasm of his body. I savored his smooth, slippery head, sucking it softly, knowing that any touch from me would elicit a sharp moan and an intense physical contraction. I loved him when he came. I loved the intensity of his response. He crawled around to collapse in my arms...just as we heard a pounding on the door.

Phillip.

David quickly changed while Phillip enigmatically pressed my emotional buttons about the evening ahead.

"You can't mind one last night. Then he's yours for life."

"This ritual means that much to you?"

"It's a guy thing. C'mon! You know he loves you. And nothing he does tonight will change that. Even if he does 'nothing' three or four times."

David appeared and called his best friend a "truly diplomatic asshole." Phillip laughed proudly, thirty-five-going-on-fifteen.

David kissed me and said, "I'm sure all I'll do is get shit-faced. Don't worry."

"I'm not worried," I said.

"I'd worry," Phillip chimed in.

"Fuck off," David told him as they walked out the door, laughing all the way to Phil's car.

Having organized the wedding with all the attention of Eisenhower planning the Invasion of Normandy, I had nothing left to do. Relatives would arrive tomorrow. Tonight, I had planned on a self-facial and an evening of laser disks. Just as I was deciding between *Godfather Part 2* and *The*

Trouble with Angels, Judith called.

"You've got ten minutes to get ready. We're going out."

"Where?"

"Not important. Get dressed. Anything casual and a push-up bra!"

Judith made me laugh. And curious. She was the boldest person I knew, a worthy namesake of the decapitating amazon of biblical lore. With no money, on a whim she would hop a jet to Paris or Paraguay, from where she'd send vivid postcards scribbled with exotic adventures. Each country held at least one lover, male or female, often both. I was as intrigued by her stories as she was by my stability.

Twenty minutes later (I *had* to do my face), I was in her cherry-red Miata, top down in the night air. All around, our senses were soothed by the scent of eucalyptus and night-blooming jasmine.

"Okay, Judi. What's this about?"

"Do you trust me?"

"You've never given me reason not to. Other than the time you dyed my hair purple before the Dexy's Midnight Runners concert. But I've forgiven you for that."

Judith smiled. "I mean it. You know I'd never hurt you. But you have to promise you'll go with what happens. I want you to forget about the wedding, about the damned bachelor party, about being the most responsible person on the planet. Just this once."

"What are we going to do? Make Carlo answer for Santino?" I was joking, to cover a rising fear that was kind of thrilling. Judith read me perfectly. She handed me a brilliantly printed red, blue, and gold Hermes silk scarf. "If you're up for this, put it on."

I touched its sensual softness. "It's beautiful," I murmured, wrapping it around my collar.

"Uh-uh," Judith frowned. "This isn't decoration. Around your eyes, please. You're not allowed to see a thing tonight."

I could have argued. Or questioned. Instead, I let her tie the fragrant silk around me, a blinding caress. She'd been my best friend since Hebrew school. How strange could things get?

Her route was circuitous enough to throw me off track. Somewhere on Mullholland I lost all sense of direction. As she drove, we talked about marriage, commitment, monogamy.

"How do you do it?" she asked. "I'm never faithful."

"When I'm in love, I'm not interested in anyone else."

"How hurt would you be if David's friends bought him sex tonight? Honestly." There was an urgency in her voice.

"Hard to say. One part of me would be devastated. Another part would know it didn't mean anything. Phillip says anything men do at bachelor parties doesn't count. I don't know."

"How do you think he'd react if you were the one partying?"

"Me?" I laughed. "Right!"

"As possessive as men are, I bet there's a part of him that would love the idea of you going wild."

I was silent. She continued, "I'm talking one night out of your entire life. One single night. I know you're hot. After seven years, David still can't keep his hands off you. You're lucky. You two have love and respect. I wish you the best marriage ever—but I still think you deserve one moment devoted to your absolute pleasure."

My head was swimming. The car stopped. I heard music in the distance. Were we at a club? A private home? "Judith, what are we doing?" I asked.

She carefully led me out of the car and took my hand.

The night air tasted sweet. My nipples strained against my blouse, less from the breeze than from a shiver of anticipation.

"I'm taking you inside. Any time you want to leave, say, 'Judith, stop,' and I'll take you home. This is a gift. Accept it."

I slowly nodded, preparing myself for whatever was waiting beyond the door.

She led me into a room scented of roses and lavender candles. I heard no voices but knew we weren't alone. She then kissed my cheek and placed a champagne flute in my hand. "I'm not out to get you drunk. This is for celebration. It's your favorite: Cristal."

I raised the delicate glass to the room I couldn't see and drank. The intoxicating liquid felt icy and good. I drank most of it, then held out the goblet to...who? It was taken by someone with a masculine scent. He moved closer, and I felt strong hands unbutton my blouse. There were soft murmurs of approval. How many were there? Men? Women? Friends? Strangers? A knot of fear leaped from my stomach to my throat. I wanted to cry, "Judith, stop!" I opened my mouth to speak...but said nothing.

I went with it.

His hands were bigger than David's, the feeling altogether new. The knot in my throat softened, began to melt, grow warm. He stepped away. I crossed my arms over my exposed breasts and the hands were back, covered in a warm oil scented of marigold and chamomile. His powerful touch worked its way down my neck, along my shoulders, down my arms. Tension melted. I became so relaxed, the sensation was so intense, that my legs grew wobbly. A second hand, softer, female, steadied me. My two protectors kept me upright. The man continued to rub his firm, oiled palms along my arms and breastbone, moving closer to my breasts, but not touching them. Mentally, I was still comparing him to David, but the scarf around my eyes, the forced anonymity, took me out of reality. This was a dream—it had to be.

My nipples, firm ripe berries, strained to be touched. Involuntarily, I pressed my upper body forward and whispered, "Please..."

The next move wasn't his. Delicate female hands crept beneath my arms to caress my breasts from behind. Caring fingers pressed into my pliant, round flesh. I had had many a massage from a female body worker, but I had never felt a woman's touch in this intimate, sensual way. It was fascinating. I thought of how David would often marvel at the softness of my skin, as I savored the sensation of her soft flesh upon mine. Its texture was so inviting, her lithe movements as deliberate as any man's, but gentle.

She moved closer, her erect nipples pressing into my back as she worked her hands over and around my sensitive, highly charged breasts. The man wrapped his arms around my back and pressed my body to his. His throbbing cock pressed into my thigh. I gasped. The woman's fingers pinched my nipple into a tiny pebble as her tongue tickled the back of my neck. Hot, moist breath bathed the folds of my ear. My head fell backward and I moaned.

My mouth open, I felt another hand—a third person's, a man's—run a fat, cold grape along my lips. With my tongue, I popped it into my mouth, taking his finger in as well. I sucked him, then pulled away to bite into the chubby, ripe fruit.

A fourth person—a woman? by now my senses were too overloaded for me to think clearly—was removing my pants and running her soft cheek—yes it was a woman—down my legs. She used her lips and teeth to kiss and nip my flesh as she traveled. I was so hot, so wet, I didn't know where to turn or who to touch—which perhaps was the point.

Four sets of hands, four pairs of lips, four centers of gravity were too much for me. My legs turned to jelly and I fell to the floor. My—what were they? who were they?—my companions cradled me and put me down on some sort of cushiony chaise lounge. I was gasping, panting, reaching my arms out to one, to all, wanting more, much more, desiring sensation, needing to know where it would go, how far I could take it, how much I could feel. Any sense of guilt was absent. If I had any regret, it was that David wasn't there to share it with me, to see me like this, to enjoy for himself this sort of unworldly attention.

My arms wrapped around yet another body, this one familiar as her cologne, the aptly named Chaos. It was Judith whose tender naked flesh touched mine, whose lips pressed against my mouth, whose hungry tongue traveled over my lips and past my teeth, who gave me my first sweet hot woman kiss, my first kiss in ages from anyone other than David. My toe was being sucked, my other foot kneaded, a soft mouth was locked on my left breast, and inquisitive fingers were playing in and around my pubic hair. It was thrilling, immeasurably erotic. And yet my energy went into this kiss, this wild, soft, sucking fuck of an embrace.

"I'm so happy," she whispered. "Accept the pleasure and know that I love you, my friend, and always will."

No one else kissed my lips that night. No cock entered me. I was massaged, tickled, fingered, squeezed, and bathed in champagne that was licked from every inch of my body; I came more times than I can possibly recall. I remember the electric sparks ignited when one of the women rubbed her nipples against mine. I can still feel the explosive orgasm brought about when the first man double-fingered me, one digit dipped within my steamy lower lips, another just penetrating my ass. I will never forget the sensation of those juicy grapes being slowly, teasingly inserted in my dripping cunt, then fished out by an insistent, insatiable female tongue. I remember every quiver, every touch, every moan and shake. And I remember Judith's kiss.

Later, Judith drove me home. Dawn was breaking. In my driveway, she removed the blindfold.

"Are you okay with this?" she asked with concern. "Don't lie."

I couldn't speak. I looked into her eyes and nodded. A look of relief crossed her face.

"Get some sleep. You're getting married in about thirty-six hours. 'Here comes the bride' and all that."

We both caught the inadvertent pun and smiled. "Thank you," I said and got out of the car. She blew me a kiss and drove off.

I entered the house. David was asleep. I crept into bed and inched as far to the edge as possible. He awoke, turned over, and cradled me in his arms.

"How was your night?" he asked groggily.

I wanted to tell him but didn't have the words. As I hemmed and hawed, he broke in.

"Judith told me her idea last week."

"You knew? And didn't say anything?"

"Why? To give you 'permission'? This wasn't my decision to make; it was yours. I don't want to be with anyone else after tomorrow, and I hope you feel the same way." I nodded. "I love that you had an adventure. Someday I hope you'll tell me everything."

I relaxed into his arms. "Tell me about the bachelor party."

"I will. Some other time."

We embraced, yawned, and fell asleep as the sun rose on our last unmarried sabbath.

Shabbos Mitzvah for a Jewish Princess

Sarah Leder

It was Friday. Tonight would be *Shabbos* and Princess
would rest. That is, her heart would rest, not her body.

They would be together. It always brought a smile to
her face when she thought about how the ancient rabbis
said it's a *mitzvah* to make love on *Shabbos*. They should
only know. What would they have thought? They probably
would have been horrified and turned on at the same time.
The quintessential exhibitionist, she would have enjoyed
having them watch. Maybe her sex life would have merited
a tractate of Talmud. The ancient rabbis could have dis-
cussed it, objectifying her, making her a sex object. Which
she, of course, would have loved.

There actually is a precedent for such voyeurism in the
Talmud. As it is written, one student hid under his rabbi's
bed while the rabbi made love to his wife. The rabbi caught
his student and asked him what he thought he was doing
there. The student seriously answered: "It is a matter of
Torah and I need to learn." From this we learn that there are
holy ways to make love, that it is important to learn these

ways, and that one of the ways to learn is through voyeurism.

Shabbos was coming and Princess had much to do to prepare herself for the Sabbath and for her lover, whom she called Daddy. She'd never quite recovered from having been raised a Jewish American Princess. The "Feminist Thought Police" admonished her not to refer to herself as a JAP and a spoiled brat, but being the spoiled brat that she was, she told them that she would "fuckin' call herself whatever she fuckin' wanted to." They abandoned her as a lost cause, and good riddance to them. She figured that when those feminists died, they would find themselves in heaven with all the Christian fundamentalists. Then she would finally be left alone in peace, somewhere else, where all the fun people got to go. She was convinced that the rabbis were indeed fun people and that for sure they would be there, wherever that was.

She was definitely a brat, badly in need of being put in her place. Judaism focuses on particularity and distinctiveness and on the notion that everything and everyone has its proper time and place. How true that was for her! She knew where her place was; on her knees. She was disappointed that Jews didn't kneel the way Catholics, Muslims, and Buddhists did. She knew in her heart that those ancient rabbis would have understood; much more so in fact, than the so-called modern feminists.

When she first started using the term *sadomasochism*, she was engaged in a very boring conversation with another woman, who expressed the opinion that it was a very misleading term. Our politically incorrect spoiled brat had a difficult time discussing this dryly and intellectually, because she was getting wet and just wanted to do it. Her strengths had always been her honesty and her willingness to be true to herself, even if the truth were unpopular. She took pride in that. Some time later, she was quite surprised to find out that the term sadomasochism was not inappropriate and misleading after all—when she realized how much she liked being hurt and that there were wonderful people out there who liked hurting people who wanted it. They were called sadists and she was called a masochist. As her ex-girlfriend used to say after hanging out with a bunch of leather dykes: "Nice girls!"

When Princess was coming out into the scene, exploring the lesbian S/M community, she joined a women's S/M support group. At one of her first meetings, she sat next to a very hot woman wearing a low-cut leotard, skin-tight blue jeans, and the highest heels she had ever seen in her whole life, with a big knife stuck in one of her boots. Princess could hardly look at this woman, who took her breath away. Who was she? At the meeting break, she asked someone, "Who is that woman?"

"She's a professional." Princess was duly impressed—such a sexy woman, and educated, too.

"Is she a doctor or a lawyer?" Princess asked.

The woman looked strangely at Princess and repeated, "No, she's a professional."

Princess knew there was something she wasn't getting. She felt stupid but asked, "What kind of professional?"

The woman replied incredulously, "She's a dominatrix." Princess still didn't get it. She dumbly persisted because she wanted to understand and feebly inquired, "What's a dominatrix?" The woman sighed and said with amazement, "She's a professional dominant."

"Oh," Princess said, the lightbulb finally going off in her head, "that kind of professional." It was at moments like this that she realized the whole world wasn't Jewish.

It's really a wonderful thing when you find your place—when you find out who you truly are and where you belong. And of course, it is even more wonderful when you find a companion, a soul mate: someone with whom you can travel to that place. Princess wryly recalled her mother's wisdom, often uninvitedly passed along to her in her childhood: "Princess, honey, I'm telling you, there's someone for everyone."

Everyone has their *bashert*, that is, their one and only, the one meant for them. In her search for her *bashert*, Princess held on to that wisdom with pious and passionate faith and hope. She had always been religious, even as a little girl. Now that she was a grown woman, she often liked to feel as though she were still a little girl: daddy's little girl. Like how it really used to be. She liked to pretend that she was a princess, a princess who made love to her prince. Now, I ask you, do you know of a better time to do so than *Shabbos?* Of course not!

Her mother had also told her, "God helps those who help themselves." That was how Princess had met Daddy several years earlier. Princess had decided that she'd better take matters into her own hands if her Prince was ever going to come. So she placed a personal ad in the local dyke newspaper and, lo and behold, Daddy responded to it. Princess had been afraid that no one would respond and was sure that everyone would think she was out of her mind. But she had taken a chance and, boy, was she glad. The ad read:

One-of-a-kind cute religious Jewish lesbian, into the scene. I'm femme bottom, you're butch top. We're both professionals (like a doctor or a lawyer) and love to learn Torah. On Shabbos, *we* bentsch licht *before going to the play party. If you wear leather but never on Yom Kippur and the dominance and submission of*

Halacha *turns you on, then maybe I could be your Princess and you might let me call you Daddy.*

Princess smiled, remembering that ad and how they'd met, but then her mind returned to the present. She stopped thinking about her happy memories and thought about this *Shabbos*, the one that was coming soon. Preparation and anticipation were crucial to both a good scene and a good *Shabbos*. For *Shabbos*, the house must be cleaned, and a white tablecloth, with shiny candlesticks and fresh flowers, placed on the table. The food must be precooked and the *challah* and Sabbath wine also on the table. Our heroine, our pious slutty little girl, prepared herself. She showered and readied herself mentally, mostly by clearing her mind of everyday worries and routine. Fresh sheets on the bed, fresh flowers.

She dressed herself for her Daddy. Daddy liked it when she made herself pretty. Tonight our little girl chose a very low-cut leather bra that barely covered her; with the flick of a finger, she could be exposed. It suited our little girl's modest nature. Jewish women are supposed to dress modestly, but not when they are alone with their husbands. But our Princess was sometimes shy, even with her Daddy. Once her desire overcame her shyness, she would be able to let go.

It was also her desire to please her master, to show that she could submit and give over her will, lose her self-consciousness. Daddy respected her submission and Daddy had earned her trust. Our little girl continued to dress. The important principle here was accessibility and vulnerability. She put on a garter belt and stockings and no underwear. Then she put on a skirt, one with buttons down the front, one that could open easily. She chose a simple button-down blouse, put on some makeup and her "fuck-me pumps." She was now ready and waiting for Daddy.

When the bell rang and Princess opened the door, Daddy was standing there—but she wasn't alone. There was another woman with her, someone Princess had never met.

"I have invited an old friend to join us for *Shabbos*," Daddy said, not asking if it was all right with our little girl; Daddy and our little girl both knew that Daddy could do whatever she wanted. That was the way our little girl wanted it and that was the way Daddy wanted it too. The more our little girl was surprised and the more she was able to go along with whatever Daddy wanted and did, the greater was her opportunity to show how submissive and pleasing she could be. This made our little girl very happy. She didn't always need to understand her Daddy; she just worried that she might not be able to obey. But Daddy was always kind and understanding, never expecting perfection or total obedience. She just expected that Princess would do her best, and she was forever turned on by Princess's desire to submit and to please her. This made Daddy happy. Happy and wet. That was the covenantal relationship between them. One was top and one was bottom, but they were equal partners in a negotiated relationship. Princess took to heart what the Jewish people said to God at Sinai when they promised to observe and submit to all the commandments: "We will do, then we will understand." That was the guiding religious principle of our little girl's sex life.

Princess was now introduced to this old friend, a handsome, strong woman about their age, probably in her early forties. Princess took the woman's coat, a new, soft, expensive-looking red leather jacket. She inhaled the smell and touch of the leather. It comforted and soothed her, giving her something to do while she tried to remember to breathe.

Princess looked up at her, and the handsome woman stared back, looking her directly in the eye. The woman wasn't unkind, but she did not smile, and her look was powerful and self-possessed. That hard, strong look went right to Princess's cunt. Princess blushed, looking away. She was scared, but excited, flushed, and expectant.

I'm in for it, Princess thought. *They are both going to take me.* And then the *Shabbos* hostess in her said, "Good thing I cooked some extra food."

Daddy told Princess to make some drinks and bring them into the living room. Princess did so and then didn't know what to do with herself. Being ignored made her anxious, but she didn't feel abandoned. She knew that soon enough, maybe even before she was ready, she would become the center of attention.

After some time, Daddy looked at Princess, gesturing with her eyes and hand for Princess to come over. Daddy told Princess to kneel before her, took out the collar, and placed it around her neck. With the click of the lock, they locked eyes. Daddy kissed Princess forcefully on the lips, and Princess moaned. Such was their ritual, which made very explicit that which was already understood. Princess belonged to Daddy. She was Daddy's slave and Daddy would have her way with her. Princess's job was to anticipate Daddy's needs and wants and to open herself up and to bend her will to Daddy's. It's kind of like how the Christians say in their prayer, "Our father...not my will but thy will be done." Princess was perpetually perplexed as to why others didn't see all the sexiness in the dominance and submission of organized religion.

Daddy continued her conversation with her friend. While Daddy talked and Princess was kneeling in front of her, Daddy slipped her hand onto Princess's nipple. Princess looked down and closed her eyes, focusing on Daddy's fingers. Daddy squeezed harder and harder. Princess knew that the only thing that would stop her from pressing harder was a scream. But she didn't want to scream. She wanted Daddy to hurt her as much as possible. She not only liked the pain, she required it. It was the grease that made her wheels go round. She held on for what seemed like a long time, and all that effort kept her from screaming until maybe only two seconds later than if she hadn't tried not to scream at all. But Daddy knew she tried to hold on, and that's what mattered. Daddy patted her tenderly on the head, the same way a loving owner pats a dog's head. Princess kissed Daddy's hand. She rubbed her cheek against Daddy's hand and moaned with pleasure. It never ceased to amaze Princess how the pain turned into intense pleasure.

Daddy told Princess to look up at the handsome woman, and she obeyed, while Daddy caressed her nipples. Princess felt vulnerable and exposed, two feelings that drove her wild. She was being forced to show this stranger her passion, while the stranger stared at and enjoyed her embarrassment. They began to discuss her.

"She is very well behaved, well trained, a good girl, very versatile and can take a lot of pain," Daddy bragged. "What's your pleasure?"

"Let's send her out of the room so that she doesn't hear our discussion," replied the stranger. "Didn't you tell me that you like to surprise her? Do you mind? After all, she belongs to you."

Daddy laughed. "Ah, but you are my guest and an old friend. I want to be hospitable. I seem to be in a mean mood tonight. It's probably my good spirits as a result of unexpectedly meeting you again after all this time. It's been a while since I brought someone home with me. And you and I have never co-topped. I think you are right. We need to talk alone. Besides, I'm getting hungry. We should eat before we play."

Daddy abruptly put Princess's nipples back in their place and ordered her to go into the kitchen and get ready to serve dinner. "We are going to talk privately and when we are done talking, you will serve us dinner. Now go."

Princess liked being spoken to that way. She had long since stopped wondering why, and had stopped wondering if it meant there might be something wrong with her. She got dinner ready, using the time to collect her thoughts. She needed to prepare herself. Tonight was going to be a challenge. She was excited, but she was also scared. She found the handsome woman incredibly attractive and very frightening, in just the way she liked being frightened. Daddy had to have known that she would feel this way. She was such a good and considerate lover.

"I generally cane her quite a bit," Daddy told her friend. "She likes the stinging feeling and besides, that's my specialty. Whips are okay, but I generally use them as a warm-up, if I feel like using a warm-up. With canes, I like to cut her skin and see her bleed. It's very pretty. I don't usually restrain her. I order her to be still, and I enjoy seeing her wiggle. That way I can punish her for moving, if I want to. But I can restrain her, if you'd prefer it."

"The main thing I want to do is something that would be hard for her," said the stranger. "I'm also in a mean sort of mood tonight, probably for the same reason as you. It's so good to see you. Princess embarrasses pretty easily, doesn't she? It's sort of cute. Would it be okay to push her a little?

I kind of would like to see her get really scared and break down a bit. Doesn't that sound like fun?"

Daddy now remembered why she liked this old friend so much and realized how much she'd missed her. She looked at her tenderly and, without thinking, kissed her old lover deeply on the lips. "I've missed you, you son of a bitch, I didn't realize till now how much. Don't disappear on me like that again."

"It's good to be back," the woman responded.

"The very thing that Princess likes is also what scares her. She likes to be objectified and exposed. That makes her feel disoriented, and then she loses control. She is shy and slutty all at the same time. It is kinda cute, but more important, it's hot. She tries to figure out what's going on, knowing that in the end, it's none of her business and certainly not under her control. What's important isn't so much what we do to her, but that we make sure we embarrass her and make her give in to us. If we talk about her instead of to her, that'll get her going. I can see that she is very attracted to you, yet afraid of you. She is trying to figure out the nature of our relationship. We can fuck with her, teasing her by not letting her know who we are to each other. That kind of teasing will torture her wonderfully. How about if I give her to you and you have temporary ownership? I will assist you in her torture. That will terrify and thrill her and would be great fun for me as well."

The handsome woman's eyes welled up. "God, I've missed you. I never met anyone as romantic as you. You really know how to treat a girl."

Daddy smiled and sighed. They hugged. "Let's go eat dinner. We'll eat quickly, and let's not eat too much. Wouldn't want to mess with our sex drives. Let's be quiet over dinner and make her nervous with anticipation. Then, let's let into her and have some fun. Tonight's going to be a good *Shabbos*."

"What's with this *Shabbos* stuff?" the visitor asked.

"Oh it's this Jewish stuff that Princess is into. She's got her S/M all mixed in with traditional Judaism. It's actually pretty cool and kinky. I enjoy it quite a bit. You know I'm Jewish, but I never knew how much fun it could be until I met her. *Shabbos* is the Yiddish way of saying Sabbath and *Shabbat* is the Hebrew way. Princess uses them both. It's a day for rest and rejuvenation, a time for eating, sleeping, and fucking. You're not supposed to worry on *Shabbos,* and it's a time when you stop doing, doing, doing. We are supposed to remember that we are not here just to accomplish things but also to enjoy God's creation. Part of that enjoyment is to take pleasure in our bodies. Early Christianity trashed Jews for being so into the body. The Romans called us 'lazy' because we took a day off. Jews have been into eating and fucking for thousands of years. I'm telling you, it's a fun religion. It just hasn't gotten good press."

Princess had thought about investigating the issue of whether using canes on *Shabbos* would be *halachically* forbidden. She had also thought about looking into whether cutting the skin might not be allowed because it could be considered creating something (also forbidden on *Shabbos*). But she eventually decided not to investigate it, because she had no intention of giving it up should it turn out to be forbidden. As an Orthodox rabbi friend of hers once told her, "If you are going to do what you want to do anyway, whether it is allowed or forbidden, then don't ask. Because once you ask and you are told that it is forbidden, it is very poor form and extremely disrespectful and rude to the rabbinic authority you questioned not to follow his ruling." Since S/M is about respecting limits and other people's needs and feelings, she decided to leave that whole issue alone. Anyway, where would she find a rabbinic authority she could tell this to without being perceived as a nasty weirdo? She sighed, wishing she knew an S/M rabbi.

Dinner was served. Princess got more and more nervous as Daddy and her friend ate quietly, without saying a word. Silence always made Princess nervous. Finally, her lover took her aside and told her to calm down. "You're getting yourself all worked up for nothing. You're no good to anyone, including yourself, if you exhaust yourself with anxiety. You know I would never cause you any harm. You know I love you and this is all supposed to be fun. So for crying out loud, just breathe. Go lie down and rest. Maybe I'll come get you and maybe I won't. Too much anticipation is too much of a good thing." Daddy kissed her on the forehead and ordered, "Now go."

Princess was disappointed, but also relieved. She plopped down on the bed and turned out the light. Soon, she was fast asleep.

Princess woke with a start. She was lying on her stomach. She started to move her right arm and suddenly felt the coldness of a chain against her skin. She slowly tried to move her other arm and her legs. She was spread-eagled and heard the slight jingle of chains. She was restrained. She remembered to breathe. She felt the stinging and burning sensation several times in quick succession before she let out a whimper.

"I think she's awake now." said Daddy.

The chains were immediately undone and Daddy barked at Princess, "Go pee and brush your teeth and get back here immediately."

Princess jumped up and did as she was told. She returned and was pushed onto the bed, face down.

"Will you keep still, or do I have to restrain you?" Daddy demanded.

"Please restrain me, Daddy." And it was done. The stinging of the cane came again and again. Unable to move, Princess showed her compliance by lifting her ass to meet the blows. She let out whimpers, trying not to scream. Her breathing grew shallow. The blows stopped and she felt a hand caressing her bottom. The pain changed, spread to wetness between her legs, and she sighed.

The two dominants laughed. Princess felt embarrassed. The many times her lover had told her she wasn't laughing at her but with her didn't seem to make a difference. She kept her mouth shut, lying there, feeling herself the object of scorn.

Daddy knelt in front of her, looking Princess in the eye. "How's my little girl doing?" she asked.

"So-so," Princess replied honestly. "I'm self-conscious, worrying about how I'm doing, trying to relax."

Daddy's voice hardened. "When I'm done with you, slut, you won't be worried about it."

Princess shuddered, but a strange calm came over her and she began to relax. The chains were removed, a blindfold was put on, and a pair of hands turned her onto her back. She assumed it was Daddy, but a horrible thought crossed her mind. There were two women in the room and she couldn't be absolutely sure whose hands those were. She repeated to herself like a mantra, "You belong to Daddy and you have given yourself to her. Your job is to obey her. It doesn't matter whose hands are touching you. It's all for her pleasure, and it's all her."

She drew in her breath and sighed. She felt two fingers on her right nipple, and then those fingers were pulling on her nipple ring. The pleasure shot through her body, landing on her cunt. Another hand was spreading lube between her legs, and then she felt the dildo. If a dildo was being worn by her lover, she always called it a cock. But this one was free-form, attached to a hand, so it was still a dildo. In one quick motion, the hand pushed it in. Princess cried out, finally letting out a scream.

"Did we hurt you, little girl?" asked Daddy sarcastically.

"Yes Daddy, you hurt me. Thank you for hurting me, Daddy."

"Oh, so you like being hurt, little girl?"

Princess whispered, "Yes Daddy, I like being hurt. Especially by you." Daddy whispered back in her ear, "It wasn't me, little girl. It wasn't me."

"It's all you, Daddy. It's all you."

Suddenly, the blindfold was pulled off. Princess found herself staring at the handsome visitor and could see that she was fucking her. The woman looked her in the eye and said, "Honey, I'm the one fucking you. Open up, cunt."

Princess closed her eyes.

"Open your godamn eyes and look at her," Daddy yelled. "Show some manners, bitch." Princess obediently looked into the woman's eyes, as though she were staring into blue space. The woman fucked her hard. Princess was in that wonderful-awful place of total discomfort and total pleasure.

The woman was hurting her and pleasuring her. She wanted to run away, yet she knew she had been born to follow orders. The woman slapped her on the cheek. "Bitch, I heard you were well trained. Your master told you to look at me. Don't embarrass your owner."

Again that strange calm overtook her; Princess relaxed and entered the pain. The dildo came out and the woman put a glove on her big hand. Hands with short nails, no nail polish and no rings. Lesbian hands.

The woman fucked her with her whole hand. Daddy was sitting on the bed and had Princess's head on her lap, playing with her nipples and caressing her hair. Princess wanted to look up at Daddy but knew that would displease her. She focused on opening up her cunt and letting the woman in as much as she could. This was a woman whose name she did not even know, a woman she had never even kissed. She felt like a whore, but if that's what Daddy wanted, then it was what she wanted, too.

But Princess was scared. As much as she opened, the fucking hand was hurting her, tearing at her insides. In a way, she didn't like being hurt simply because it hurt. This confused her, because she also liked it because it hurt. After all this time, she still didn't quite get it. She knew that she wanted to show Daddy what she was willing to take for her; it was kind of a masochistic macho. But she was also embarrassed. What kind of a person would allow herself to be given to a stranger in such a fashion? Princess thought too much, fought too much. Why was it so hard for her to trust and just enter the pain? After all, it inevitably transformed itself into intense, almost unspeakable pleasure. She had met some masochists who claimed to actually enjoy the pain itself, but Princess considered herself to be a more ordinary sort of masochist. She primarily liked the pain because of the transformation that it brought. The trust that was necessary was really threefold. First and foremost, she trusted that Daddy knew what she was doing and that she would not actually cause her any real damage. The second part was to trust the process of how the body worked, to trust that pain would turn into pleasure. And last, she needed to trust herself; trusting that she would still be there for herself even if she were to let go; rather, especially if she were to let go. She loved the New Testament proclamation "He who loses himself shall find himself." Wasn't that what S/M was all about?

"Just be the pain and breathe," she coached herself. Focusing on her breath, she slowed it down. The woman pulled out her thumb and began alternating between pumping in and out of her cunt and circling her clit with her thumb. Princess's pleasure mounted. The woman was in tune with her. She could tell that Princess had finally given herself over to the pain and to her. When she relaxed and entered the pain, the hurt felt good. The clitoral stimulation was getting her close to the edge. She knew better than to come without asking for and getting permission. Thinking about that made her wetter. She sure was wired funny. Princess politely asked the woman if it would please her if she came.

"The insolent bitch wants to come," the woman sneered, addressing Daddy.

"Please don't think of me that way," Princess begged. "Please."

"Please shut up," the woman ordered. "Shut up and don't come." The woman continued to tease her by circling her clit while Daddy squeezed her nipples. Princess gritted her teeth, pleading with her eyes for the woman to let her come. Princess was afraid she'd mess up by coming without permission. Then she felt herself growing angry for having been put in this impossible position. She knew that the woman was purposely pushing her buttons, trying to make her angry.

Finally, the woman said softly, almost kindly, "Honey, now you can come for me." Princess felt ashamed of her anger. She hoped the woman hadn't noticed. She made a mental note to herself that she really needed to work on learning to trust and be a better girl.

When Princess came, it was with a loud scream, while staring into the woman's eyes. Afterward, she felt naked and cold. She shivered. Then Daddy covered her nakedness with a warm blanket, scooped her up in her arms, held her tightly, and cooed in her ear, "Good girl. Daddy's proud of her good girl."

Princess didn't look at Daddy now that she had the chance. She held on tight as the tears started to flow. It was over for now. She felt fulfilled. She had heard the words she had wanted to hear. Daddy was pleased. That was all that mattered. After a few moments, Daddy ran her fingers through Princess's hair, kissing away her tears and saying in a kindly whisper, "Good *Shabbos*, good girl."

Princess caught her breath, kissed her Daddy on the cheek, and answered: "Good *Shabbos*, Daddy, good *Shabbos*."

The Nanny of Ravenscroft

Joyce Moye

I tapped on Jack's bedroom door, even though it was open. I don't know when I had stopped thinking of him as Mr. Mainhardt, or even as John Mainhardt.

He was sitting in one of the two chairs that flanked the fireplace, cradling a brandy snifter. His feet were propped up on a tufted hassock upholstered in the same chintz as the chairs. A fire crackled on the hearth, the flickering light throwing reddish shadows on the satin lapels of his dressing gown.

I pictured the cozy domestic scene this must have been when Valerie was alive: husband and wife, relaxing after a long day, gazing silently into the flames and listening to music.

Handel's *Royal Fireworks* was playing.

"Come in," he said, without looking in my direction. He nodded toward the vacant chair. "Have a seat."

Glancing down at my fleece robe, the hem of my flannel nightie, and the oversized bunny-rabbit slippers peeping from beneath, I felt more out of place than usual. Valerie Mainhardt would have worn peach lace.

"She's asleep," I said as I sat. "I think her fever's broken."

"Here," he said wearily as he passed the brandy snifter to me. "Drink this."

We were comrades-in-arms, surveying the littered battlefield at the end of a long fight. He rose, walked over to the small oak credenza where a silver tray held a crystal decanter and several more crystal glasses, and poured himself another brandy.

"Earaches are hell," he said.

"Especially on parents," I observed wryly.

The biting, pungent fumes made my eyes smart as I took a sip of the liquor. Old, expensive cognac seared my throat and burned its way down.

He raised his glass in a salute as he returned to his chair. A smile hovered around the corners of his mouth. "I take it nannies are immune?"

"I'm not experienced enough to be immune." I gave him a self-deprecating grin.

We probably weren't talking about Precious anymore. In the last few months, we had arrived at a place where friendly banter rippled just above the surface tension of deeper waters.

Uneasy, I tried to change the subject. "Do you always have a fire going in here, even in the summer?"

Whenever he was home, neatly laid logs burned discreetly on the hearths of Ravenscroft.

His eyes sparkled with mischief. "Always."

When had I begun to think of him as handsome? His massive head, pockmarked complexion, and broken nose were not the Hollywood ideal.

"Why the infatuation with burning logs?" I asked.

"Why?" he repeated absently as he stared at the red-hot coals. He knocked back half the contents of the brandy snifter and gave me a detached smile. "When my parents died, my grandfather sent me to a spartan English boarding school. A first-rate place, as they like to say." The smile faded as his words trailed off. "It was one of those public schools that purport to turn boys into men with a regimen of frigid showers and freezing dorm rooms."

His expression hardened. The memories I had dredged up were far from happy ones.

"And being from California," I said quickly, wishing to undo what I had started, "you never could get warm."

"Sort of." Flashing an ironic grin, he visibly relaxed. "I was born in New York, actually. When I returned to the States, I'd never heard of surfing."

I made a tsking sound. "And they say American culture is universal."

He lifted one black eyebrow, and my insides began a slow meltdown.

"*They* say a lot of things," he said in a low, earthy tone.

I probably shouldn't have had more than one sip of brandy; the alcohol had turned my tired limbs to Jell-O and my brains to mush. Lulled by the crackling fire and the enveloping sense of intimacy, I foolishly ventured beyond my depth.

"Kim told me that when Celeste first came to work here, she entered the house on her hands and knees. Is that true?"

As soon as I'd said it, I was sorry. I really didn't want to know about my predecessor's kinky habits, and I most especially didn't want to know if she'd been his mistress.

"Would you like it to be true?" He watched me over the rim of his brandy snifter.

"I...I don't know," I replied, thrown off balance. "Forget I asked." I waved a hand, as if the gesture could erase my question. "I was just curious." I shrugged and gave him a wry grin. "You would think I'd be used to Kim's weird sense of humor by now."

I was offering a graceful way out. For both of us. Or perhaps it was only a cowardly, last-ditch effort on my part to find an escape.

"Curiosity is good," he said softly.

The heat in his languid gaze was so intense that I had to turn away. I glanced around the lovely room, desperate to change the subject.

Though Valerie had been dead for three years, her presence still hovered in every corner of Ravenscroft. It struck me that I was jealous not of Celeste but of Valerie's ghost. To hide my feelings, I made what I thought was a casual remark.

"It must have been nice, sitting here in the evening when Mrs. Mainhardt was alive, maybe playing cards across the hassock."

"Cards?" He gave me an odd, incredulous look.

When I nodded innocently, he barked out a coarse laugh.

With the toe of his slipper, he shoved the hassock in my direction.

"The seat lifts up. Want to look inside?" *Step into my parlor, said the spider to the fly.*

How could I turn down a dare to open Pandora's box? Cautiously, I raised the hinged top. I don't know what I expected would jump out.

He chuckled. "Nothing in there will bite you."

By the fire's glow, I studied the contents of the hidden caché. There were lengths of silk and bits of leather, and here and there a glint of metal. I had no idea what any of it was for.

I decided that the Mainhardts must have had a

remarkable marriage. More than ever, I envied Valerie with her porcelain loveliness and erotic sophistication.

"Quite a toy chest," I said, hoping I sounded blasé. Primly rearranging my fleece robe across my knees, I glanced down at the bunny-rabbit slippers. The sight reminded me that I was the nanny, and I'd never be as cosmopolitan as Valerie Mainhardt.

"Hah!" Behind his crude laugh, I glimpsed something darker.

I was in way, way over my head. The only thing to do was brazen it out.

Reaching into the hassock, I extracted a strip of black velvet with some Velcro on the ends. A brass chain attached the velvet to a second strip of velvet. I held the fabric aloft, dangling it from my thumb and forefinger like a soggy piece of ribbon.

"What's this?" I tried to sound nonchalant.

His eyes crinkled at the outer corners as if he were enjoying a private joke.

"Handcuffs," he said and waited for my reaction.

"Ugh," I replied. I didn't try to conceal my distaste. "I don't believe in tying up women. Macho fantasies are a turn-off."

I was no longer interested in impressing him. I was ready to call it a night, hand him the brandy snifter, and return to my room.

He smiled sardonically. "How do you feel about tying up men?"

My mouth fell open. I couldn't think of a clever retort.

He stood, and, as if drawn by a magnet, I stood right along with him. We were no more than a few inches apart. Pulsating currents filled the space between us. I raised my face, expecting to be kissed.

"Want to see how they work?" His cognac-scented breath warmed my cheek.

I nodded mutely.

He bared one forearm, shoving back the silky sleeve of his robe. His thick wrist was covered with black curly hairs, fine hairs that would tickle in all the right places.

"It's very simple," he said, the liquid heat in his voice numbing my reason.

He wound the length of velvet around his left wrist, the way someone would don a watchband, and pressed the Velcro ends together.

"You fasten the other one." He held out his free arm and the empty handcuff.

Without thinking, I complied.

"Now I'm your captive."

A white-hot thrill raced from my knees to my neck. Never before had a man offered to be my slave, to do whatever I wanted. Heck, I'd never even been asked *what* I wanted.

"Well?" His black eyes twinkled. He tipped his head to one side, clearly curious as to how I'd react. And, just as clearly, trusting me. A heady surge of power washed over me.

I sputtered out a nervous laugh. "I've never done this before."

Chuckling, he raised his arms and dropped his bound hands behind my back, imprisoning me within his embrace. Through fleece and flannel, I could feel his desire.

"But you're curious," he murmured.

"Yes," I said, my breath caught in the back of my throat. "Very curious."

His cologne enveloped me; a distinctive mixture of lime and cardamom probably custom-blended for him in some place like Milan or Manila.

My pulse hammered in my ears. I could scarcely breathe. My heart was pounding so loudly that I was sure he could hear it. If he kissed me now, I knew I wouldn't care who was the prisoner and who was the jailer. Nor who was the employer and who was the employee. The Jewish nanny and the wealthy WASP.

He brushed his lips across mine. "This is called 'topping from below.' "

"Oh," I croaked, not daring to ask what that meant.

His kiss was gentle—and drugging. As his lips molded mine, the *Royal Fireworks* melded with the hiss and sizzle coming from the hearth.

I pushed against the wall of his chest.

"We shouldn't do this," I said, struggling for air.

"Whatever you say." There was a mischievous gleam in his eyes. He relaxed his grip, allowing his arms to hang loosely at my hips. "You're in charge."

Some tiny, inner devil, lurking within some dark crevice of my brain, assured me that I could handle this. After all, I was in control. I could take things as far as I wished and no farther.

For how long had I wanted to run my fingers through Jack Mainhardt's wavy, black hair? How long had I ached to slide my hands around the back of his neck and draw him down to me? How long had I hungered to kiss him until our lips were swollen with desire? *You can have all that,* the little voice said. And I listened, even though I knew there would be consequences.

"Kiss me," I ordered.

"My pleasure." He obeyed with ravenous zeal, although his arms remained slack at my hips.

"Hold me tighter," I demanded. Raising his hands, he crushed me to him.

As his mouth found mine once more, my palms roamed his satin lapels with feverish need—but his dressing gown was not what I needed to touch.

I opened the buttons of his pajama top and explored the hard contours of his muscles, surprisingly well defined for someone who spent hours at a desk. I wondered fleetingly if he worked out. There were so many things I didn't know about Jack Mainhardt, though I lived under his roof. I slithered my nails through the coiled hair between his pectorals.

"Take off your pajamas," I breathed.

One elegant eyebrow quirked upward. "I'd love to comply, darling, but I may need a bit of help."

"Yes, right," I said, feeling idiotic.

With a soft chuckle, he raised his arms over my head and extricated me from his embrace. His eyes danced with amusement as he held out his handcuffed wrists to me.

"If I release you," I teased, "is the game over?" More than anything, I didn't want him to retreat back into that brooding shell of his.

He gave me an angelic smile and shook his head, his bound arms still outstretched in my direction.

"There is only one rule to this game," he said in a husky baritone. "Well, two rules. The first rule is that no one leaves anyone else tied up when they exit the room."

"And the second rule?"

"The second rule is that no one does anything without the other person's consent."

The fire popped and sparked. I was drowning in brimstone. "But how will…"

He kissed the tip of my nose. "I'll tell you."

As though he could read my racing thoughts, he raised his manacled wrists and rubbed his knuckles along my cheek.

"And *you'll* tell *me*," he said softly.

As I gauged the ermine depths of his gaze, I realized I

was hopelessly in love with Jack Mainhardt. An impossible attachment, given the nature of our relationship. I was the nanny, nothing more. I glanced away to hide my feelings— and found myself staring at his enormous bed.

The immense, scrolled-ironwork headboard and footboard were connected by an overhead frame, which, I surmised, had once been intended to support mosquito netting. I could envision the whole thing gracing a plantation bedroom in the muggy jungles of Malaysia. And I could imagine a dozen different ways a lover could be shackled to that bed. I had seen the enormous bed before, of course, but this was the first time I was seeing its carnal possibilities.

"It's late," I said, remembering where I was—and with whom.

I turned to go. He caught my hand with both of his.

"You just broke the first rule." His heavy baritone was hypnotic.

"Oh," I said in a tiny voice, embarrassed. With my eyes focused on the thick green carpeting, I reached for the Velcro bindings. "I forgot."

"It's okay, darling." The droll humor was unmistakable. "It's your first time."

Too mortified to meet his gaze, I unfastened the handcuffs and headed for the door.

I was at the threshold when I heard his rasped plea.

"Don't go, Michelle. Please."

His hoarse entreaty, filled with loneliness and longing, drew me back into the room.

"Don't talk," I ordered, joking.

He barked out a laugh, his eyes smoldering with anticipation, but he spoke not a word as I led him toward the iron-bound bed.

"Lie down." I pointed a finger. For a moment, I pictured myself holding a small whip. Undoubtedly, there was such a toy in the depths of the hassock, but I banished the image as ludicrous.

He lay on his back, his arms outstretched above his head. Patient. Obedient. The cuffs still around one wrist.

I slipped the chain portion behind an iron curlicue and reshackled his other wrist. One corner of his mouth twitched.

A horizontal man with a vertical need. I chose to ignore what was obvious as I toed off my bunny slippers, climbed onto the bed, and stretched out beside him.

As I had been wanting to do for a long time, I caressed his cratered face, stroked his wide shoulders, fondled his abdomen. I trailed my lips along his collarbone.

His chin nudged my flannel nightgown. "Are you planning to take that off?"

"You aren't supposed to speak," I said with a prim sniff. "I'm in charge here."

He laughed. A deep, rolling belly laugh that I'd never heard before. And one that I wanted to hear again and again.

"You have a real aptitude for this, Miss Cutler."

"Didn't I just tell you to be quiet?" I couldn't suppress my own laughter. He nodded, his eyes still moist from laughing. Giggles threatened to overtake us.

"Hush," I snickered. "This will never do."

"Take off your blasted flannel nightie, Michelle."

Our gazes locked until our laughter burned away, turned to steam like the evaporating puddles from a summer shower when the scalding sun reappears.

I sat up and, kneeling, yanked off my robe and nightgown. I was naked before I realized he was still wearing his silk pajamas.

"These have to go," I muttered, the time for banter long past.

As I dragged off his pajama bottoms, he raised his hips to assist me, which not incidentally brought a certain aroused part of his anatomy closer to my lips. With a look, I warned him not to ask for anything.

He closed his eyes, and a shudder ran through his body. I saw him straining for control, but he refrained from giving me instructions. Even if he had, it wouldn't have mattered, because I knew what *I* wanted. I settled down astride him.

"Oh, God, Michelle." He let out a raw groan.

I stifled the rest of his moan with a kiss, a kiss that went on and on. Mindless with need, I teased my nipples against the springy hairs of his chest as the rise and fall of my pelvis matched the thrust of his hips.

He gasped for air. "Michelle...release me."

I shook my head, refusing. My mouth recaptured his.

Together, we were soaring toward the sun. And when I burst into flames, I didn't know whether I'd found heaven or entered hell.

Afterward, I lay crumpled against his chest, sated and drifting toward sleep. He kissed the top of my head.

"Release me," he whispered.

"Give me one good reason." I rose up on one elbow and fluttered my eyelashes at him.

"I want to hold you," he said simply.

"Aw, geez." Tears prickled behind my lids and threatened to spill over. "Now you're playing dirty."

Determined not to let him see me cry, I swallowed against the lump in my throat and undid the Velcro.

His arms settled around me.

"There. That's better." With a contented sigh, he snuggled closer.

We were peacefully entwined when I heard Precious call my name. I glanced toward the door, and with dismay, saw it was still ajar.

"Oh, shit," I said as reality intruded.

Pierced

Emma Holly

New York frightened her.

Victoria waited at La Guardia, praying her older brother hadn't forgotten to meet her flight. Henry was the original absentminded professor, but she'd called to remind him just last night. She checked her watch again and swung her carry-on into her other hand, afraid to set it down amid this teeming anthill of humanity. In the twenty minutes since she'd landed, she'd seen three scruffy men digging through the trash receptacles. Her palms were sweating, as was the small of her back. And now a scary, skinny man with bleached blonde hair and at least eight gold hoops marching up his right ear was staring at her, his eyes squinted and his head awry.

Her face burning, she looked away. She just knew the man was going to approach her. Sure enough, determined footsteps cut across the bustle. *Oh, God,* she thought. *What do I do?* She tightened her grip on her bag and started moving toward the nearest courtesy desk.

"Hey," said a voice. She spun around so fast she hit

herself in the thigh with her bag. It was him: the tall, skinny blonde. A funny sound issued from her throat, a whimper of fear. The blonde touched her hair, cupping the silky brown strands with surprising gentleness. "I didn't mean to startle you. Are you Victoria?"

"Yes," she said with what was left of her breath.

The man's grin slashed across his bony face. "I'm Pierce Freeman, Henry's lodger. Your brother got stuck in a faculty meeting and asked me to meet you."

"Oh," she said, relief making her dizzy. "I thought—"

He laughed, a bigger laugh than she'd have thought a skinny person could make. "I know. You should have seen your face. I'm sorry I'm late. The subway was hell. Some guy took a dive off the platform and held everything up until they cleared him off."

Victoria went cold. Clearly, she'd left small-town Minnesota behind. She was still shaking by the time they collected her luggage, so Pierce insisted they take a cab.

"I have money," she said, because he looked as if he could barely afford a meal, much less a taxi. He grinned and said his mother had taught him better than that. He certainly seemed capable. He told the driver exactly which streets to take to avoid the worst traffic, and he did it in such a mild, friendly manner that the man didn't take offense.

She watched him as he and the driver struck up a conversation. His earrings glinted in the bright June sun. The bottom one was a little Egyptian ankh that trembled when he moved. His jeans were so ripped she could see one long thigh muscle through the tears, at least until she wrenched her gaze away. His bleached hair looked even stranger in the daylight, rough and stiff with a circle of black roots. He had beautiful hands, though; graceful, long-fingered, pale. She noticed all his nails were bitten to the quick.

"So," he said, turning sideways to face her. "What do you think of the city so far?"

She hadn't the faintest idea.

Henry still wasn't home, so Pierce took her to a place called Caribe in Greenwich Village. Amid plastic palms and garish tropical murals, they ate the most delicious West Indian food Victoria had ever tasted. Also the only West Indian food. The amount Pierce was able to shovel in astounded her. He must have the metabolism of a blast furnace.

He seemed to know something of her history already. In fact, he showed more interest in her mother's summer in AA rehab than Henry had. Pierce's familiarity with the Twelve-Step program unnerved her until he explained that his father had been through Narcotics Anonymous.

"But he's back at the top of his game," he said, waving a forkful of curried goat. "The best nip-and-tuck man in New York."

"Your father is a plastic surgeon?"

"Yup." His dark eyes crinkled with amusement. "So I never will understand why he objects to my body modifications."

Was that what they called it? Body modifications? Then she thought, *Gracious, what if he's got more "modifications" than I can see?*

The question preyed on her during the long walk home. Though the streets were filled with freakier freaks than Pierce, her eyes kept sliding to the spots he might have embellished. His nipples formed small bumps beneath his purple tie-dyed shirt. They were intriguingly erect, but uninformative as far as jewelry went. She couldn't make out his navel, and it was too embarrassing to stare for long at the soft bulge at the crotch of his jeans. She'd heard of men wearing tiny barbells in the tip of their penis, supposedly to increase their partner's pleasure.

The possibility brought the side of her thumb to her teeth.

"Don't," said Pierce, pulling it away. "Biting your nails is a terrible habit."

"You ought to know," she said.

The words came out sharper than she'd intended, but he laughed and squeezed her hand. He didn't let go, either, though it was hot and they were both sweating.

Victoria felt safer almost at once. Pierce was no football player, but he obviously knew his way around. Her neck unkinked and her eyes wandered, and suddenly she noticed how interesting her surroundings were. Mixed among the freaks were brainy-looking college students and foreign people and women so stylish she felt quite the frump in her baggy walking shorts. Her eyes widened at a shop selling nothing but black leather corsets. Pierce stopped to let her look.

"How old are you, anyway?" he asked.

Victoria blushed. "Nineteen next week."

"Nineteen, huh?" Pierce looked thoughtful, but he didn't release her hand.

Victoria didn't realize she was aroused until they returned to Henry's air-conditioned apartment, where everything dried but her panties. Then she became aware of the persistent pulsing between her legs. A fresh trickle of moisture slid from her pussy. She was almost afraid to hug her brother for fear he'd smell her lust. She needn't have worried. Henry hardly ever noticed anything. He pulled her into his stocky chest and stroked her long hair down her back.

"Look at you," he said. "All grown up and pretty as a picture."

Victoria smiled at the old-fashioned compliment. "I see you grew a beard. Very distinguished." Actually, he looked ten years older, more like thirty-six than twenty-six.

He patted the bushy growth, then slapped his belly. "That's not all I've grown. I'm hoping you'll drag me running with you while you're here this summer."

"You could have come running with me," Pierce said.

Even Henry heard the hurt in his voice. He slapped Pierce's shoulder. "Forget it, Mr. Speedy. You're too fast for me."

Pierce hung his head and grinned, both mollified and sheepish.

Oh, dear, she thought. *I wonder if he's gay.*

Pierce wasn't gay. Pierce had three girlfriends, possibly four. Two of them looked so much alike that Victoria couldn't decide if they were one woman or two. All the girlfriends wore black and had harsh, multicolored hair. Henry called them the Goths. He teased Pierce about them like a fond uncle. He didn't notice how being reminded of their existence made his little sister squirm.

Victoria couldn't stop thinking about Pierce. She'd bumped into him one morning coming out of the bathroom without his shirt. He did have nipple rings, two gold half-hoops hanging from protruding red nubs. *Goodness gracious,* she'd thought, *was the man always erect?*

"You're gonna catch flies if you don't close your mouth," he teased, but he was blushing, and a second later he said, in a strangely husky voice, "Want to touch them?"

She wasn't sure he was serious, so she laughed nervously and turned away. She couldn't resist casting a glance over her shoulder, though. The sight of his naked back tore the breath from her lungs. It was all lean, smooth, fanning muscle: a man's back, a gorgeous back. His shoulders were broader than she'd expected, and his tight little runner's butt—oh! Her mouth watered and sensation swelled like steam between her legs. She'd had to finger herself to climax in the shower.

Ever since, she'd known she had a case for him. She hated those girlfriends. Stupid, gum-cracking, bolt-nosed Goths. Victoria's room, formerly Henry's study and still jumbled with papers and blue books, was wedged between the two men's. Sometimes when the Goths stayed over, she'd hear them moaning with pleasure. Pierce never made a sound. Pierce was a gentleman.

Pierce was far too good for the likes of them.

Victoria stopped in her tracks. Pierce's door was open. He lay on his bed reading, his long, pale body draped in nothing but a pair of black satin running shorts. His room was painted a deep, earthy red. An odd leather harness dangled from his bedpost. No doubt the Goths knew for sure, but those straps looked just the right size for binding a man's private parts. Victoria's nipples tightened beneath her tank-style T-shirt. She leaned against the doorjamb to hide them.

"How on earth did you and Henry meet?" she asked.

Pierce looked up from *The History of the Celts*. His butt clenched as his legs shifted on the sheets. Victoria wondered if he might be getting an erection.

"I answered his ad for a roommate. We're both Mets fans. And I don't smoke."

Victoria shook her head. Men were the most peculiar creatures.

They went running together for the first time. Henry

had a rare hangover from a faculty party the night before, so Pierce volunteered to keep her company. She could tell he was a serious runner. He set a steady, ground-eating pace, slow for her sake but more challenging than her usual. The morning was misty and muggy; New York in shades of gray.

She wiped her face on her sleeve as they dodged a garbage truck backing out of an alley. Pierce stripped his shirt off and tucked it in the back of his running shorts. Victoria nearly tripped. A thin gold chain connected his nipple rings.

"Doesn't that hurt?" she asked, nodding at the bouncing links.

He grinned. "Nah. It's light. It feels sexy."

Sexy, she thought, the mere word making her pussy swell. She tried to concentrate on not huffing and puffing, but a block farther she couldn't keep her question inside. "Why did you do it?"

"You mean get pierced?"

She nodded.

Without breaking stride, he swung his arms to loosen his shoulders. "I wanted to claim myself."

"I'm surprised you needed to. You don't seem like you could belong to anyone but yourself."

"Then I guess it's working." With a wink and a grin, he sprinted to the top of the hill. Victoria had a heckuva time keeping up.

Henry found her a job at the university, tutoring students in English who weren't quite up to Columbia's standards. The first day, Victoria was so nervous she threw up, but three out of her four students were eager and friendly, and the one who wasn't dropped out after the second week.

One of them, a shy Korean woman who was pursuing

a Ph.D. in physics, invited Victoria to her aunt's house for dinner. There she was served the most amazing twelve-course meal she'd ever eaten. She loved everything, even the weird stuff. Naturally, the relatives, most of whom spoke broken English, loved her. Her only regret was that Pierce wasn't there to share the experience. Since he wasn't and since the aunt forced her to admit she didn't have a boyfriend, one of Sung Kim's cousins asked her out—her first date in over a year.

She was nervous, but not too nervous to enjoy herself. When the quiet young man kissed her good night, she enjoyed that, too.

It just didn't set off fireworks the way Pierce's bare chest did.

Inside, she found him watching TV in the darkened living room, an old Ingrid Bergman film. The sound was barely audible. His head turned toward her. "Have a nice time?"

"Yes," she said. "We went to Little Italy."

He kept looking at her. The TV flickered on his nipple rings. Something about his stare struck her as strange. Then she put her finger on it. "I didn't know you wore glasses."

He removed the shiny circles and folded them. "I don't."

"No, I like them."

He put them back on. They both laughed.

"I'm glad you had a nice time. A pretty girl like you should go out more often."

Victoria twisted her purse strap around her hands. That sounded like something Henry would say. Pierce hooked one leg up on the couch. Force of habit made her eyes slide to his crotch. Oh, God. He was hard. A giant bulge pushed up against the well-worn seam. She could actually make out the separate swell of the glans. Did he mean for her to see? Or did he assume she couldn't?

"He didn't get fresh, did he?" he asked.

When her brain lurched into motion, she laughed. Now he really sounded like Henry. Feeling bold, she tossed her head. "No fresher than I wanted him to be."

"Brat," said Pierce, and beaned her with a balled-up sweaty sock.

Victoria slept with it under her pillow.

The three of them went to the Peking Duck House to celebrate Henry getting tenure. Victoria wasn't surprised. Whatever Henry set his mind on, he always rose to the top. Sometimes she wished she had his direction. Despite that niggle of worry, she was pleased to see him happy. Besides, he had dreams enough for both of them. He stabbed the air with his chopsticks.

"You ought to transfer to Columbia," he said. "No point in you cowering in Minnesota now that you've got your feet wet here. I know the chair of the English department. He'd accept you in a snap. If you've got to be an English major, you might as well be one somewhere that counts."

Victoria rolled her eyes at his snobbery, but Pierce leaned forward. "Don't pressure her, Henry. If she likes the University of Minnesota, that makes it count for her."

Henry seemed genuinely surprised by the scold. He pressed his hand over his wide brown tie. "Sorry, Sis. I didn't mean to offend. I just want you to know you could do better and you don't have to be scared to try. I'd be happy to have you stay with me."

Victoria saw that he meant it. She didn't know many brothers who'd make such an offer. "Thank you, Henry. That means a lot to me. I promise I'll think about it."

Pierce looked down at his crispy pork and vegetables, his lips pressed together as if he dared not say another word. She hoped he didn't mind the thought of her staying on.

Pierce owned a shop in the Village. Whenever Victoria asked about it, both he and Henry became vague. Then, one Saturday, Pierce accidentally left the key to his stock room on the kitchen table. Victoria was the only one available to bring it to him.

Immensely proud of herself, she took the subway to the address he gave her without making a single mistake. Her grin broke out as soon as she saw the shop. She knew it. Pierce owned a combination condom-fetish store. A saddle sat on a pedestal in the display window. Its horn was a large wooden dildo. A pair of thigh-high boots were positioned beneath the saddle, giving the illusion of an invisible Valkyrie riding an invisible horse across a sea of foil-covered rubbers.

Pierce stuck his head out the door. "You can stop laughing now."

She pressed her palms to her cheeks. "Just tell me when I can stop blushing."

She wouldn't hand over the key until he agreed to give her the grand tour. The shop was cramped, but it seemed to be prospering. The shelves were well stocked and it was far cleaner than Henry's apartment. Her blush ebbing and swelling, she nodded at the whips and handcuffs and shiny rubber maids' costumes. All in all, peculiar though the inventory was, the place had a friendly feel; Pierce's doing, she was sure. She stopped at a shelf toward the back. Pierce stood behind her. Perhaps it was her imagination, but his body heat seemed to beat at her in waves.

"What are these?" she asked, lifting a series of marble-sized balls linked by a silken cord.

Pierce coughed. "Those are anal beads."

"Ah," said Victoria, though she wasn't much the wiser. Pierce's breath stirred her hair; it felt warm and harried. Victoria stopped breathing altogether. Her body swayed backward. Her shoulder brushed his chest, bumping the hard little ring hidden beneath his black T-shirt.

"Lord Almighty," Pierce said and strode into the stock room.

A month before, Victoria wouldn't have had the nerve to follow him, but she was a New Yorker now, at least for the summer, and New York women feared nothing.

She found him standing with arms braced on the window that overlooked the alley behind the shop. He wore black leather today, like his Goths. A thick silver chain looped down from each side pocket. His uniform, she guessed. His butt looked so adorable she wanted to drop to her knees and bite it. He was breathing like a man about to submerge in deep water.

"What's wrong?" she asked, even though the fearless, womanly part of her knew.

He turned and the look in his eyes pierced her soul—a mixture of longing and misery she'd never thought to inspire.

"What is it?" she said, softer yet. She stepped closer, close enough to touch.

He reached for her. He wrapped his hands around her shoulders, his eyes searching hers.

"Your brother's going to kill me," he said, and kissed her.

The shape and feel of his lips enthralled her: thin, mobile, and wide. His tongue pressed inward and found an eager welcome. He moaned down her throat. A tingle swept her from scalp to toe. She felt as if she'd never been kissed before. This was a kiss. This was a mouth. The right taste, the right pressure, the right mix of gentleness and lust. His hands released her shoulders to clasp her face, one palm deafening each ear. He tipped her head just so, and the kiss perfected itself.

Her paralysis broke. She took his waist between her hands, kneading the hard block of muscle on either side. His feet sidled hers, as he shuffled closer with another lovely moan. She swept her thumbs down his hipbones, daring that much, daring to touch the edge of the taut, sloping leather that crossed his straining crotch.

When she brushed his balls, he cursed and grabbed her wrist. With a grunt of pleasure, he molded her palm over his erection. He turned his head, kissing her desperately now, then clutched her buttocks and thrust as if he meant to crush her fingers between them. She was just gathering the nerve to thrust back when he shoved away and wiped his mouth on the back of his arm.

"I'm sorry," he said, his hand shaking, his face crimson. "I shouldn't have done that." He turned to the window. "It won't happen again. Henry would kill me."

"Henry likes you," she managed to say.

"That doesn't mean he wants me making out with his baby sister."

Was that all she was? Henry's baby sister? She left without saying good-bye.

One of the Goths came over that night, the one with the purple hair and the tongue piercing. Victoria buried her head in her pillow and cried. She never heard how loudly the Goth moaned or if this time, God forbid, Pierce moaned back.

She woke at two, according to her travel clock. Her face was hot, her eyes sandpaper rough under their lids.

She'd look a fright tomorrow if she didn't get the swelling down. She pressed her ear to the door and held her breath but heard nothing. Heart beating, she tiptoed to the kitchen for ice. The sight of Pierce's beloved cookie dough ice cream tightened her throat. Wistfully, she touched the dented lid. A mattress creaked. Victoria jerked her hand back as if she'd been burned. Diving for the light switch, she plastered herself to the wall before anyone could see her.

The door to Pierce's bedroom opened. She peeked into the living room. Pierce and the Goth came out. He wore silk boxers. The Goth was dressed, or what passed for dressed to her.

"Promise you'll call?" she said.

Pierce murmured something indecipherable. The Goth grabbed his ears and pulled him in for a kiss so assertive Victoria could only marvel. When it ended, Pierce steered the Goth toward the door and saw her out.

Then he headed for the kitchen. Victoria's heart skittered into double overdrive as he passed within inches of her. He didn't bother with the light but walked straight to the freezer. He pulled out his ice cream, then dug a spoon from the drawer he and Henry kept in the worst jumble she'd ever seen. He leaned against the counter to eat it straight from the carton.

"Fuck," he said between heaping spoonfuls. "Fucking, fucking fuck."

Victoria felt like a spy. And a coward. "I thought only women did this," she said.

The spoon clattered across the floor, but Pierce managed to catch the ice cream. "Geez, Victoria, you scared me."

She stepped away from the wall. Her heart was pounding in her throat, but she kept moving. "You mean now or this afternoon?"

He froze in the act of retrieving his spoon. He straightened. Victoria heard his breathing change, grow faster, shallower. "This afternoon I scared me."

She stopped a foot away from him. She touched his chest with her fingertips, brushing the edge of his areola with her thumbs.

"Victoria," he said, but she wouldn't let him silence her.

"I want you, Pierce. I've wanted you almost since I met you."

"Oh, God," he said to the ceiling, and it really did sound like a prayer. He set the ice cream down. His chest rose and fell under her hand. "To hell with it. I can't keep my hands off you a minute longer. Come with me and I'll give you as much of me as you can take."

He drew her by the hand to his room. She remembered that first evening in the Village with their hands linked and swinging, being so frightened and feeling so safe because of him. She felt the same way now. With Pierce to guide her, she knew she wouldn't lose her way.

He closed the door before he turned on the light. He stroked her hair behind her ears with his long, beautiful hands. "We have to be quiet. I don't want to upset your brother."

She nodded. They both knew how stuffy Henry could be.

He bent down until they matched eye levels. "Are you sure about this? I'm not like the other boys you know. I don't even have a real job."

"You own your own store. Isn't that real?"

"I own a condom store. I sell whips and chains."

She put her hands on his shoulders. "Is that you talking, or your father?"

He sighed and embraced her, pressing her cheek into his warm, hard chest. "With you, I don't always know who

I am, except it's different than with anyone else."

"Is that bad?"

"No." He kissed her hair. "No." His heart sped up beneath her ear. His voice dropped to a whisper. "I'm crazy about you, Vic."

"Even though I don't wear black?" she said, thrilling to the little nickname. "Even though I don't know much about, um, sex?"

He pushed back from her, his grin splitting his narrow face, his dark brows climbing his pale forehead. "I wouldn't worry about that. You're about to get a very enthusiastic teacher."

He kissed her in earnest then, and this kiss was even better than the one in his shop because she knew it wouldn't end so quickly. He stroked her back and her body arched. When she buried her fingers in his hair, it was so much softer than she'd expected that she had to rake her nails back and forth.

"Oh, yes," he sighed between kisses. "Touch me, Vic. Touch me."

She didn't start to shake until she undressed, and that was only because she'd never been naked in front of a man before. And not a whole lot of women, either.

Pierce sat on his rumpled double bed and watched her through heavy-lidded eyes. Finally her body was bare, the body that persisted in staying round and soft no matter how often she ran. His gaze traveled over her. He rubbed the center of his nearly hairless chest. "You're even more beautiful than I imagined."

She laughed because it was such a corny thing to say.

"I mean it," he said and tugged her onto the bed on top of him. As they kissed, he wriggled and twisted and then he was naked, too.

She gasped as his burning length strafed her thigh, then pushed up on her arms to look at him. *Oh, my*, she thought. His cock was long and red and thicker in the middle than it was at either end. It rose from a tangled thatch as black as the roots of his hair. His penis wasn't pierced, but he did sport a tattoo, a Chinese dragon whose head started at his prominent hip and whose tail tickled the base of his shaft. She traced its outline with her fingers, then cupped his balls. They were plump and round and compact enough to fit in one hand. Victoria loved the feel of them. She rippled her fingers over their swell. When she looked up, Pierce's eyes were closed.

"More?" she said.

"Please," he rasped.

She straddled his body and stroked his cock in her loosely closed fist, not sure what to do but aware that she was pleasing him. He covered her bottom with his graceful hands and drew slow circles with his fingertips. The circles drew closer and closer to her sex. He touched one lip and slid inward on a trickle of cream.

"Don't," she said.

He stopped and opened his eyes, his gaze focusing with an effort. "What's wrong?"

"There's something I want to do first." She bent until her breath fanned his sharp, beringed nipple. "Tell me if this hurts."

She took him in her mouth, ring and nipple both. His back bowed upward.

"Mm," he said. "Yes, suck me."

She sucked him, slowly, wetly, adoring his textures: the smooth, firm nipple, the cold, hard ring. She used her tongue to catch the hoop, gently increasing the pressure. He shivered and clutched her hips.

"Christ, I can feel that to my toes."

She switched sides and he groaned, his hips jerking sharply upward, his cock squashing her thigh. He rolled her beneath him while he fumbled in his night table drawer. His watch fell to the dusty floorboards.

"I'm not rushing," he said, ripping open one of the packets he'd spilled onto the pillow. "I'm just preparing."

She ran her hands up and down his ribs. "I don't mind. I'm ready."

His cock jumped at her words, dressed now in transparent blue latex. He rolled the condom's hem over his base and squeezed himself in a way that delighted her. He shook his head. "Not yet, honey. You're not quite ready yet."

He eased her onto the pillows and spread her legs, soothing her with strokes and kisses before he lowered his head. He opened her with his fingers and explored her, licking every nook and fold and rubbing his whole face over her sex as if he wanted to wallow in her scent. Then he suckled her clit.

A low cry caught in her throat. *Oh, my,* she thought. *Oh, my.* Now she knew what the Goths had been moaning about. His mouth pulled and rubbed and licked all at the same time. The combined sensation was so intense it was almost painful. With his hands, he kneaded her mound and inner thighs, pressing her flesh deep into the bone and finding spots she hadn't known were sensitive. Her legs began to thrash. He had to hold them down with his elbows. He hummed as if he found her delicious. *Oh,* she thought, tears springing to her eyes. *Oh, my God.* She clasped his head, lightly, not wanting to jar him. Her finger found his line of earrings and ruffled them. A shiver rolled across his shoulders. She came and she came and finally had to push him away because she couldn't bear any more.

"Okay?" he panted, crawling up her body. He settled between her thighs, his cock hot and long across her thatch. "Are you okay?"

She hugged him tight with arms and thighs and neck. "Yes, yes. Thank you."

He stroked her hip. "Can I come inside?"

"Yes," she said, and reached down to open herself for him.

He stiffened when the head of his cock found her barrier. "Oh, Vic." His eyes filled.

"It's all right. I want you to be the first."

"Vic. Honey." His Adam's apple bobbed. He didn't move except to stroke her hair back from her brow. "I want you to know I broke up with Sharon tonight. I broke up with all of them."

"You didn't have to do that."

He blinked hard and hid his face in the pillow by her cheek. "Oh, God, Vic. Yes, I did."

She kissed his jaw. "I'm glad," she whispered.

He snorted a laugh and rose back on his elbows. A single wet streak marked his cheek. It awed her more than anything that had gone before. His hips nudged forward, stretching the fragile barrier. "Are you ready?"

She nodded and bit her lower lip. He held her gaze and pushed. It only stung for a moment, and then there was nothing but the pleasure of his body gliding slowly, deeply into hers.

"That is so nice," she said when he was fully seated.

He smiled and she wondered when his strange, bony face had grown so beautiful. She ruffled his earrings again and his cock quivered inside her.

"Brat," he said.

"Yes, but I'm your brat."

That brought a different look to his eyes, a serious look. "Honey, if this is your walk on the wild side, I don't want to know."

She kissed his chin. "It's not."

He pulled back and rocked slowly forward. "I hope not."

"It isn't." She inhaled sharply because his movement was doing lovely things to her.

"Like that?" he asked, doing it again from a slightly different angle. She moaned and clutched him. He rocked her like that, up on his elbows, watching every expression that crossed her face, repeating the motions he thought she liked, deepening them, quickening them.

She gritted her teeth. "I'm not coming without you."

He laughed and nipped her earlobe.

"I'm not." She slid her hands down his spine and dug her fingers into his buttocks.

"Geez," he gasped, but she could tell he didn't mind the pinching pain because his hips moved faster and his breath came harder. Still on his elbows, his hands curled over her chest to squeeze her breasts.

I'm going to make him moan, she vowed. Just this once, he'll moan. She leaned up and kissed his breastbone. His fingers tightened on her breasts. His torso twisted, placing one nipple before her mouth. She flicked the ring with her tongue and bounced it up and down.

"Do it," he said, and she sucked him in.

He jerked and groaned. She laughed, the ring still caught in her teeth. Almost good enough. Almost loud enough. She reached between his legs to cup his swinging balls. She circled them the way she thought the harness might, two fingers and a thumb and a palm to roll the rest.

This time his moan was all she could have wished for. He muffled it on her shoulder.

"Vic," he said, his hand squirming down her belly to find her clit. "Vic, hurry."

She let all her hunger free then, squeezing him, touching him, writhing like a wildcat on the sweaty sheets. This was Pierce in her arms. These were Pierce's long, hard legs, Pierce's arching spine, Pierce's rough, sharp jaw. She wanted it all. She loved it all. She moaned his name. Her body clenched on his pumping cock, a long, shuddering embrace. What a sweet, sweet ache. Their mouths grappled in a sloppy, panting kiss. Her orgasm hit a second peak and then he, too, let the fury loose, silently, eyes screwed shut, gasping for air as he slung in hard and spasmed.

"Geez," he said, sinking down, his face nuzzling hers. "Geez. No. Don't hug me yet. Wait a sec." He held the base of the rubber as he withdrew from her, carefully, with a little sigh of reluctance at the final parting.

"Let me," she said and gingerly peeled off the sheath. Once she had it free, she held it to the light and let it swing back and forth. The milky pool of fluid fascinated her. This was Pierce's semen. She'd made him shoot it.

Laughing, he took the rubber and tossed it in the trash. They wriggled together with his arm around her back and her head on his chest. He pulled the sheet over them. They traded sighs.

"What are you thinking?" he asked.

"I thought women were supposed to ask that."

He tweaked her nose. "You can ask me later. Now talk."

"I'm thinking this summer is going to be way too short."

"Ah," he said, a pleased sound. He kissed her forehead.

"Don't worry, honey. If it's meant to be, it'll work out, and if not, we'll have the best summer of our lives."

She smiled and flipped his right nipple ring to face the other way. He didn't press, but she knew he wanted her to stay as much as Henry did. Her brother would throw a fit when he found out they were sleeping together, but he did like Pierce, and he would come around. She hugged her new lover's ribs. What an adventure this was. Anything might happen if she stayed. Who knew how Pierce would change her? How New York would change her? Oh, she was just so happy she'd fallen in love!

"So, Pierce," she said as she drew one finger down his belly. "What would you like to teach me next?"

"No, no, no." His eyes sparkled as he shook his head. "What would *you* like to teach *me?*"

Out of Brooklyn

Robin Bernstein

"My cat," she says. "Say hello to Tammy, Buttface." Lonnie waves the cat's paw at me. "Buttface is sixteen," she says. "Same as me."

"And me." We're on our knees in her doorway, stroking the cat's gold back. Then Lonnie scoops her up and closes the door behind us.

The apartment faces east, but heavy drapes split the sun into spears.

"My mom thinks light is bad for the furniture," Lonnie explains, as she cranks the blinds open, "but I think she just likes to sit in the dark after those fluorescent lights at the hospital."

When the drapes part, what was warm and muted becomes sharp and splendid.

"You want orange juice, maybe?"

"Sure."

The kitchen is dusty yellow, and the table has only two chairs. Lonnie lifts a pile of newspapers off one of them So I can sit on it.

"So, what's new since yesterday?" she asks. "Any revelations?"

"Well, I called Emma."

"And?"

"And got my ear yakked off about that senior, the glorious Melissa Kellogg."

Lonnie whistles. "Your friend has some crush."

"Emma?" The thought hadn't occurred to me.

"Is Melissa straight?"

"Oh, sure, she's got some boyfriend in college."

"Anyone ever actually meet this boyfriend?"

I laugh. "Oh, come on."

"I'm just assessing your friend's chances."

"It wouldn't make a difference. Emma is most emphatically straight."

"With a capital 'Q.' "

Orange juice shoots out my nose.

"Oh, I'm sorry," I say, but the words send another whoosh of juice out my nose. I'm mopping and Lonnie's laughing and blowing bubbles with her straw.

"Relax. OJ is good for the formica."

"You're so kind. My parents are neatniks. Although lately they're away so much, they wouldn't notice if I drove a dump truck through the den."

"Your parents are weird."

"Listen to this. Yesterday I tell my mother the springs are poking out of the couch. So she hands me her credit card and tells me to go pick out a new one and have it delivered. So I say, 'Don't you want to help me choose?' And she says, 'Nah, I trust your taste. Besides, you're the only one who really uses the living room.' "

"Bizarre. But at least they treat you like an adult."

"Your mom is okay on that."

"Yeah, that's true. All right, we each get a B+ in parent selection. So, did you pick out a couch yet?"

"No."

"How about today?"

"You want to spend the day shopping?"

"Sure, I never bought a couch before. It'll be an adventure."

"Hardly," I say, but I let her talk me into it. Shopping is one of the things I hate most in the world, but anything is fun with Lonnie.

They sell everything on Kings Highway, so that's where we run. We're charging down Coney Island Avenue, laughing and playing slalom through the strolling Chasidic families. When we get to Kings Highway, though, we realize that we can't buy anything there on Saturday. All the best stores are closed, with big signs in Hebrew: *"Shomer Shabbat."* Guard the Sabbath.

"Nuts," says Lonnie. "You wanna go to Manhattan? They're all atheists there."

"You are corrupting me," I say. "I've never had a need that Brooklyn couldn't fill."

"That's faintly pathetic."

We hop the subway to Macy's. The car is half empty, and Lonnie amuses herself by swinging around the pole. I want her to sit with me, but she's got ants in her pants. Suddenly I have this awful feeling she's going to lead me, running, all over Manhattan. We're going to engage in all sorts of sophisticated, fascinating activities at top speed, and never have time to really talk.

"Hey Lonnie," I say, "you're not going to drag me into some café where you get a thimble of cappuccino for $3.50, are you?"

"No." She stops swinging. "Do I look like a yuppie?"

She resumes swinging.

In Macy's, Lonnie hops from one couch to another, throwing herself into odd poses.

"Eating potato chips," she announces while lying on her back with an imaginary bowl on her stomach, feet flung over the sofa's arm.

"Watching *Dracula*." She leaps onto another couch, curling herself as small as possible into the soft crook.

I say, "Recovering from long day," and droop myself over a couch's back, tush in the air. Lonnie is darting all over the store. I've never seen her quite this hyper.

Then I realize that in fact I've barely seen her at all, except for a few odd moments captured between classes: all our long conversations have been over the telephone.

"Hey Lonnie," I ask, "do you always run around like this? I mean, what do you do while we talk on the phone?"

She climbs out of a paisley couch. "What?"

I repeat myself.

"Oh, " she says, reddening a bit. "Well, sometimes I pace a little. Or I pick at my toes, that sort of thing. What do you do?"

"Just sit, mostly.

"Oh."

"Let's just choose a couch and go." There's a price tag dangling next to my hand. I look at it. Three thousand dollars. I scream.

"Lonnie, let's get out of here."

Outside I lean into her ear and hiss, "I hate Manhattan."

"Shit!" Lonnie slams her face into her open palms. She stomps away from me, hugs herself, looks at the sky, then exhales. Finally she returns to my side.

"I'm acting like your friend Emma," she says, scrubbing her eye with her fist. "I'm running in a million directions, all of them away from you."

"No," I say, but I realize it's true: in the subway, in the store, I'd felt that familiar frustration. "It's not so bad," I say.

"It's easier over the phone, you know?" Lonnie says. "When we're just talking, it's one thing at a time." I nod, knowing what she means: we can feel one thing at a time.

"I'm sorry," Lonnie says. "I'm nervous, that's all."

"Me too."

"Sometimes I can't stand myself."

"Lonnie, you are marvelous." I lean over and gather a piece of her straight black hair between my thumb and forefinger. "You have the most gorgeous hair I've ever seen on a white girl."

She sniffs and smiles a little. "My mother says it's 'cause she read so much Eastern philosophy while she was pregnant."

"I believe it."

We hug, our breasts fitting together like gears. Then Lonnie pulls away, her eyes bright.

"Can I show you one Manhattan marvel? Just one?"

"Sure," I laugh.

"It's called the Strand," she says. "Twenty blocks downtown."

One hour and two knishes later, Lonnie ushers me into the largest bookstore I've ever seen. "Eight Miles of Books," declares the sign.

"Awestruck?" Lonnie asks.

"Awestruck," I admit.

Lonnie snakes me through twelve-foot-high shelves. "Here's the women's studies section," she says, after leading me to the rear of the store. "There's a gay section behind us, but it's mostly men."

You are truly marvelous, I think, but I don't say it again. We both turn to the wall of books and become absorbed scanning. Suddenly I feel something on my hand, something small and warm. I look down. Lonnie is nesting her hand in mine.

"Is this okay?" she asks.

"Yes," I say. We turn back to the wall, skimming titles. All I can take in, though, is the strong cable of our arms and our suspended, linked hands. From behind, we must look like the Brooklyn Bridge.

The next week our words dry up. We've emptied our childhood stories, unpacked all our secret wishes, run out of biographical data to pass along. Sometimes we find a new stream of ideas, and the talk flows like clear water. Mostly, though, I sense a thick, white mass between us—I think it's paste of chaste. Or pastity of chastity—a consciousness of curdling time. While it makes me sodden and slow, it also makes me more sure of what I want.

When conversation eludes us, Lonnie and I sing. She favors the grim, cynical musicals—*Threepenny Opera* and *Cabaret, A Little Night Music* and *Sweeney Todd*. Me, I'm a sucker for *Bye Bye Birdie* and *The Sound of Music*. Luckily, we both love Peter, Paul and Mary; The Mamas and The Papas; the Weavers. With their help, we spackle the holes in our conversations for a week. Then she invites me to her house.

I think, *What does it mean? What if I'm misinterpreting everything? Is it possible?*

And I say, "No, come to my house." Because we both know: my parents are in Montreal.

Lonnie hugs me hello and my nose pokes through the stream of her hair.

"Someday I want to see your parents," she says.

"Me too. I barely remember what they look like."

She holds up her guitar. "As promised," she says. "I brought music, too, so we can sing."

"I want to hear something you wrote."

She shrugs. "Later, maybe."

What came next? I can hardly remember. We sat on the floor and sang from the Weavers' songbook: "Follow the Drinking Gourd," "Darling Corey," "Wimoweh." Lonnie's voice was strong. Our harmonies were indestructible: pure geometry. Our voices were becoming grainy when Lonnie said, "I want to play one that's not in the book. I learned it from their reunion album."

I sat by her side and she began to play. The song had a purple-red quality, like a slow, heavy rainstorm. I couldn't really follow the words. Lonnie's eyes were closed. Then the song changed, and the words became:

There's something about the women
Something about the women
Something about the women in my life.

It circled endlessly, becoming stronger and stronger. Light poured from Lonnie's face. My body seemed to become seamless, listening to the song with recognition. It was like the first time I'd ever heard a song. A precious secret and marching band in one.

In my life, there are women,

In my life there are women, in my life.

The song closed like a heavy book, and Lonnie's eyes stayed shut. There were no words in my head. No thoughts. Just the expansiveness of a galaxy. Lonnie's eyes opened. I coasted to her lips. Touched them with my own.

It wasn't even a kiss, just a touch, but it made my insides avalanche. I felt rocks falling from my shoulders, jagged granite I hadn't even known was there. The unbelievable softness of her lips.

The guitar struck a note when it hit the floor. Lonnie didn't seem to notice. Her arms encircled me, her lips kissed me. No thoughts anywhere, only softness. Nothing dangling, wondering, worrying. Only the rightness, the absolute completeness.

Lonnie twisted away, crying in silent little beads. Frightened, I asked, "What's wrong?"

"It's just that I'm so....relieved," she said, pulling me back to her.

I felt the last boulder topple from my shoulder, and I was crying too, because I had never been myself before that moment. I had been Tammy, waiting. Now I was Tammy. All my questions, insecurities, maybes were evaporating into ghosts. In their place was fiber and feeling.

"Tammy," she named, and I was me. Our faces together, tears puddling our shirts. Everything salt. And joy. As we kissed, our crying ebbed, salt crystallized, and we became serious. My fingers wove through her hair, just as I had imagined a thousand times. Her hands on my neck, my shoulders, my back. My teeth at her ears. Her mouth on my throat. I ripped myself away.

"We gotta stop." My voice sounded like I'd just jogged a mile.

"Why?"

"Because..." I realized I had no good reason. "Because what if we get pregnant?"

Lonnie cupped my jaw in her hand. "Honey, that isn't going to happen."

"But I feel like it could."

"I'll call the Pope," Lonnie said, squeezing my hand.

The completeness I'd felt was gone, replaced by more wanting. Lonnie understood. She took my hands and drew me off the floor and onto the bed.

I swept all the dolls off my quilt in one superhuman gesture. Lonnie positioned herself in the bed, and I jumped in after her. Our arms pretzeled, we clung and kissed.

"I can't believe it's you," she said. "I'm so glad it's you."

Our whole bodies pressed together: breasts, stomachs, the tops of our thighs, even our feet. I squeezed her bony shoulders and kissed her neck. Lonnie's feet grabbed one of mine, lifting. A regular gymnast, she simultaneously parted my thighs and sprang on top of me.

I had never imagined. All my hours of pretending, of picturing—nothing came close to the fundamental rumbling I felt when Lonnie first surfed like that, her thigh a rudder between my legs. My hands stuck like starfish to her back, but soon they loosened and slid. I stroked her from shoulders to waist, feeling her ribs like ripples in a sandy riverbed.

With each stroke, I dipped my hands a little more to the side. Her hand was scrunching in my stomach, scrabbling upward like a bear cub climbing a tree. She crept up, I crept down, until each of us was at the perimeter of the other's breast, our fingers brushing around again and again.

I couldn't believe I was doing this, that I had the *right*, that she was *letting* me. That she wanted it, too. That her hand was—oh—full on my breast.

I hastened to do the same, my heart crashing.

"God," she said, and I felt her nipple ripple beneath her shirt. Then she sat up suddenly, her eyes never leaving mine. She crossed her arms, grasped the base of her shirt, and pulled up.

"My God," I said. No bra. Breasts shaped like teardrops. Her body, shoulder to waist, uninterrupted by a bra, by a bathing suit. I had the right to look. I was allowed to look. I ripped my shirt off as fast as I could. Lonnie tried to unfasten my bra, which messed up the rhythm, but eventually we got me untangled.

"Pillows," she said, caressing me with both hands. Touching her and being touched at the same time—it was like reading and eating and taking a bath all at once. Which is, of course, my favorite activity. Well, *was* my favorite activity.

"You're so soft," she said, her voice full of wonder. She knelt and kissed me from throat to belly and back again.

"Let me!" I pulled her down and tasted every naked part. It was a strange, slow ritual of faces, shoulders, hands. Her body full of shadows like the moon.

I don't know how long we rocked like that, tasting, testing. Sometimes I was half an inch tall, exploring the folds of her belly button. Other times I was fabulously large, cramped in my room like Alice in the White Rabbit's house. I never expected the fine hairs on her neck, never imagined her licking my palms. Everything I never had even wished for: it was all coming true.

I bet you're wondering if we ever took our pants off. For a while, I thought we shouldn't. It seemed frightening, messy, complicated, better left to another day. But my hands loved her hips, her hips loved my thighs, and soon the word *yes* was trumpeting through me like the sound of the *shofar*.

We stood, giggling, trying to make sense of each other's buckles and zippers. First my pants came off, then hers. Underwear and socks peeled away, and we stood, looking.

All her lines ran vertically: legs straight and white as junior slim tampons, hips hardly thicker than waist, waist barely smaller than shoulders. Her hipbones stuck out like the wings on an Edsel."You're gorgeous," she said.

I looked down at my body, full of crazy S-curves and cellulite. Rumpled and messy. When I looked back up, Lonnie was inches away, drawing me to her.

We kissed, standing, our full bodies together. I felt—I swear, I *felt* myself turning into a woman. Felt my body expand, heavy and flowing as magma. Magma—that's molten rock. What an impossible idea, that rocks can melt. What a completely impossible idea.

To Celebrate the Ordinary

Elaine Starkman

Today, the first day of autumn, we become lovers, our wetness the wetness of droplets, our noise their noise as they gently fall to the ground and into the dry soil of our neglected backyard. A day I've awaited for over twenty years, when I was the Libby who let you make our decisions, the one who agreed to stay home with three children and remained too frightened to go back to work until they were nearly teenagers. The Libby who now demands that you move under my body, that you stay here in the warmth of the covers a while longer. *No, don't leave. The children are gone. The house and chores, they can wait.*

From what place do such demands reach my lips? From my overworked mind? From this quiet after all these years? From doing work that pays, that gives me a sense of worth? Here we lie, you and I mirroring all those couples we read about in crass books, view in slick films, an outmoded statistic, still married among our newly unmarried friends.

Rain sinks into the soil. You sink into me. There's no dichotomy of mind and body; one no longer cancels the other. *"Yes,"* I say, *"oh yes,"* like Molly Bloom; the long years of denial and our ineptness are gone. I hope the sun doesn't come out; let it remain gray, quiet, soft, a late September morning with nothing to run toward or from.

Yes. The fault mine for not admitting it sooner. *Yes.* The early years of dependency when I didn't know what to ask, how to ask. The baby-making. Long, dreary years, my young self without a sense of my body other than the function of my growing womb. We barely touched. I was too placid, you, too staid, too married and responsible to be my lover. I lay on the delivery table murmuring, "I love you." After our third came that dark, unsettling feeling that lasted for months. Not yet thirty, I had to imagine lovers. I couldn't say "I love you." Even now, those words fill me with caution; I know their transience.

Images in my head: that time at Mann Ranch in Ukiah when the therapist told me, "I was fifty before I knew passion, knew how a woman's body worked." I am not yet fifty.

"Slow down; we've time today. Let's brush our teeth. Don't look at the clock. We're not going anywhere. My hair, stroke my hair, that's it. Good. Now bring a towel."

Is this chatter a fear that we could separate like Julia and Howard, our longtime friends who had everything?

My woman's body. The shock of watching this body age while my mind remains a child's mind. *Flower of the mountain.* If I will it, if I allow it.

"You use sex as a weapon, you use it to change me," you'd say. And now you're overwhelmed with *my* change, with *my* wanting to hum like a cello.

The years of child-rearing. Who knew how exhausting they'd become, how they'd tear us apart?

"Beth's dropping French."

"It's Beth's life."

Undermining me with your acceptance, making me Witch Mother to your Prince Father; Bad Mom made life easier for you.

When the children grew older, the rush, the frenzied schedule. Never any time alone. We read the sex manuals and threw them into the garbarge. Their effects lasted less than a week, then we'd be back to our old patterns while our offspring burst forth with their shocking sexuality. Let them learn to love their bodies the way we never have. Let them not mask their senses.

Our own recalcitrant years, years of ideological moves across the country, out of the country, of being caught up in separate worlds. I became less than those parts, blaming you. How I lost my wedding band in the garden, in the garbage disposal, down the toilet. A miracle flushed it back up. I wanted to rid myself of you, but wherever I'd run, I'd find pieces of you in me. Now I lose nothing, no longer run, no longer blame. I'm back where you wait for me, pre-dictable and unchanging, while both of us unlearn how alien we are even to ourselves.

Where to place this arm, eyelid against armpit, toes interlocking.

"Do you think Julia and Howard are happier now?" I finally ask.

"Never mind them."

Your teeth grind into mine, each beginning as awk-ward as the first, each ending as if we've been strung togeth-er since our births. How I know your intelligent scent, your fair skin covered with too much hair, your dry hands with the broken finger that never healed right, your nails clipped too short, the parts you hide from me.

"Tell me what you're feeling."

Your rabbinical eyes close with the dread of my insistence that you talk.

You stir. Open your eyes. Your fingers are still unsure of who they might find. Look at my new belly, these droopy little breasts that never grew. At last my body forgets my mind; it arches to its animal purpose. To celebrate the ordinary. Make my ordinariness unordinary, open my fullest, most vulnerable self to you. But don't overtake me. For this moment, I, not you, must remain the wild one, the free one in my imagination.

And now quietly you sleep again, vein pulsing in your neck. Rest. I must not need you too much. *Knee inside knee, keep me safe.* The old dependency rises, makes me want to separate. Will you become the sweet old man to my cranky old woman, the eye of our mutual respect rearing its head so differently from that of our children and their lovers?

I go to wash. I go into my separateness. The sun rises; the phone rings; the drip of rain on the roof has stopped.

The Locusts

Cara Bruce

... and when it was morning, the east wind brought the locusts. And the locusts went up over all the land of Egypt, and rested in all the coasts of Egypt. Very grievous were they; previously there had been no such locusts as they, nor shall there be such after them.
Exodus 10: 14-15

Every seventeen years they come out of the ground to feed. There are so many of them it is impossible to walk anywhere without killing them. I watch from the kitchen window as they eat all the leaves off my trees, leaving nothing but their discarded brown shells. They fly in a group to the next leaf, momentarily darkening the sky. The worst part is the noise, an incessant buzzing. The buzzing that has replaced all other sounds of life. The buzzing that I hear when I wake up, when I fall asleep, and even through the barrier of my dreams.

I turn on the faucet to get a glass of water, watching as it runs red from rust in the pipes. I imagine the metallic taste, like blood, and I look toward the locusts as if this too could be their fault. My husband is walking up the front sidewalk, his big feet crushing whirring locust bodies into the cement. His lips are drawn tightly together and I look at the clock. It is only one. I told him not to go in at all, that he wasn't ready. He merely looked at me, unsure of what else there was to do.

We buried my eldest son within a day of his death, according to Jewish law. I imagine his gravesite invisible except for brown shells. I believe their crunchy covering is keeping him warm, but I also worry that their buzzing keeps him awake.

Daniel opens the front door, brushing the bugs off his shoulders and hair. "Rachel," he says quietly. I come to greet him, opening my arms, allowing him to collapse inside me. I hold him tight, and when he pulls away I see tears in his eyes. He brings me upstairs, his hand resting heavy on my arm, weighted with grief.

We go into the bedroom and he lays me down on the bed, nuzzling his nose into my neck, planting his mouth hard upon the soft hollow of my throat. His kisses are rougher than usual and I can feel his desperation. I wrap my arms around him, scaring away the flies that have landed on his already sweaty back. His hot tears drop on my breast as he opens my denim work shirt and moves his mouth down over my bra. He kisses me through the black lace before reaching behind and unclasping it, pulling it up but not all the way off so it rests upon my chest. He lightly bites my hard nipple, massaging my tit with his hand.

His head is moving down toward the soft pillow of my

belly. He rests for a minute, inhaling my warmth; then he unbuttons my pants, pulling them down, breathing over the pubic hair that presses right up against the worn-out silk of my panties. He rips them down.

He is moving quickly; I can feel his need to taste and feel all of me. I raise my hips to him as he pushes fingers into me, up into the place where his son came from. He kisses me there, he is whispering something but I cannot hear him. I hear only the beating wings of the locusts. He pulls my clit with his mouth, licking it, sucking it. I close my eyes and reach above me, pressing back on the headboard. I push into him, attempting to match his intensity. Feeling good through my pain.

He unbuttons his dress pants and I see his cock spring out. Thirty-four years ago that cock made me pregnant, in a time before AIDS, before being careless meant only a new life, not the threat of deadly disease. He pushes into me, stretching my walls and filling me up with his throbbing prick. He goes in deeper, and again I push back. He is fucking me as if we were young: hard and fast. I open up until my entire body is cunt and I am swallowing his pulsating grief. It runs through my veins and I absorb. He thrusts again and I feel him in my stomach. He is moving and I go with him, feeling all the women before me, the pain of persecution, of epidemic, of plagues, feeling it for myself, for my husband and for my son. The locusts have covered the sun, and in the room I can see only the outline of my husband moving above me, soaking me with himself and his sorrow, allowing me to feel again, to make sure life has not stopped and that we will somehow go on. I cling to him, digging my nails into his back, closing my eyes and mixing the buzzing with my orgasm, bringing me all at once into and out of this life. I come, tightening my legs and holding on with all my might, finally allowing myself to sob.

L inguistic

Stacy Reed

Meyercurve is by definition a ghetto—its majority is the city's minority—but it's hardly a slum. It is home to many fantastically educated and affluent Jews. The Hebrew Community Center, as well as Beth Yushiddah (the largest synagogue in the state) and its academy, cast shadows on the ebbing Protestant congregations and schools, the Christian day-care centers. Meyercurve is a suburb to which Jews congregate.

They all seem to come from somewhere else: Newark, Philadelphia, Los Angeles, primarily South Africa. Older residents speak Afrikaans or Yiddish among themselves, while their children learn Hebrew. Even the least linguistically agile among us memorized the Hebrew prayers delivered in temple, especially the gracings at bar and bat mitzvahs and at the highest holy days: Rosh Hashanah, Passover, Chanukah. The majority of adults have an "M.D." or a "Ph.D." following their names, earned at prestigious institutions in the Northeast. The Protestants are mostly chemical engineers or corporate lawyers.

Though there is a tendency to form cliques, mingling is not shunned. Crossing religious lines became popular among the social, the liberal, and the curious during the early seventies. In Meyercurve, the pervading intellectual leaning contributed to inter-religious friendships, occasionally even marriage. The atmosphere nurtured assimilation and discouraged isolation by any particular constituency. In-grouping exists, and may always, but few failed to transcend it.

When we were teenagers, I doubt that any of us gave Meyercurve's social dynamics much thought, unless a straggling parent forbade inter-religious dating or warned against the allegedly insurmountable obstacles such a marriage would harbor. Most of us shrugged off these admonitions with a roll of our eyes or sarcastic laughter. We considered these forebodings prejudiced, old-school, and foolish.

Then I entered my junior year at Bellcreek High School, a public magnet school for the arts. Ms. Carlton taught history and politics to the advanced-placement crowd. The first day of school, she told us to sit anywhere we pleased, that seating was not assigned. I had not foreseen such luxury happening before college.

Ms. Carlton then instructed us to look around at our neighbors. She asked what we noticed. No one cared enough to notice anything except that, for the first time, we were sitting next to whomever we pleased.

She crushed our newly acquired "self-initiative" like a used-up cigarette.

"How many of you are Protestants?" Seven people sitting close together raised their hands shyly.

"Catholic?" Three.

The Blacks and Asians seated in their two areas began to look at one another.

"Drama students?" All five sat next to and across from each other; they raised their arms sheepishly.

"Who's Jewish?" she asked, the point already made. Nearly fifteen of us sat close together. She nodded at us sagely as the blood rose to our faces.

"This exemplifies de facto segregation," she began. We listened halfheartedly, humiliated "gifted" students who thought of ourselves as beyond what we had clearly just demonstrated. A fog of naïveté and indignance settled in the classroom. She had blown the ashes down the neat aisles, point made and taken. She'd attended Bellcreek herself, and she taught history and politics as much from personal experience as from books and lectures. And that was how we learned them.

Tuesday we sat randomly. We still knew our neighbors, and we liked them, but we could not restrain ourselves from cutting our eyes toward familiars. Still, though Ms. Carlton had exposed us, we refused to drop our ideology. We'd blast into Room 304 as if it were a cocktail party each day after the bell sounded and make straight for the person who was in some way different from ourselves. Our vehemence faded, and awkwardness quickly followed. But soon we paid little attention to who was sitting next to whom. That class became my fondest memory of high school, but I have never forgotten that first Monday's revelation, that well-deserved backhand. I doubt that any of us will.

Our mental acrobatics and gray-matter graffiti came to fruition in that room. Lessons in history and politics became secondary or supplementary instruction; a chasm separates good intentions from their realization. By the time we began studying for the SAT, we had fashioned a bridge: sloppy and risky it may have been, but the bonds held. We began learning what really counted, and how only a few things count at all. Exploring ourselves and one another quickly took priority over the *Princeton Review* and the International Baccalaureate exams.

After that first week of frantic posturing, Dirkyon Patrick began making an effort to sit next to me. If Jason Addler or David Saul sat beside me, Dirk always sat behind Jay or Dave. I knew Dirk was looking at me. I'd wonder if my dress tag had turned up or if a bra strap was showing. I was careful not to touch the back of my hair; I didn't want Dirk to know that I might possibly care about how I looked from his vantage point.

He was from Amsterdam, so he spoke perfect English by the time he immigrated to the United States at fifteen. Dirk was popular and his peers tended to glamorize him. He was the only one among us who was European. His parents were Black Irish. He had very white skin, absurdly blue eyes beneath heavy lashes, and shiny black hair cut evenly above his wide jawline. He was Catholic.

Each Friday we seated ourselves in a circle to discuss the week's current events, clipped and noted in the proper binder. Before our second week's exams were returned, Dirk had fallen into the habit of maneuvering himself next to me at the end of each week, casually setting his backpack on the side of his chair opposite mine and scooting his desk closer. Once he brushed his thigh against my knee and quickly crossed his ankles: apparently a mistake. I concentrated intensely on Ms. Carlton's mediation of a debate concerning Oliver North and fished for an insightful sentence. She averaged participation into our GPA.

I saw Dirk at parties or at Meyercurve Mall, but I seldom spoke with him outside of Room 304. Whenever we did speak, he was friendly and focused our conversation on reviewing for finals or acquiring citizenship. Dirk never invited me to his house to study, but he continued his ill-disguised flirting each Friday. His lunch began during the first half of the fourth period. Mine ended when the bell rang out the beginning of that period. Only time for an exchange of smiles in the hall.

Our senior year, Dirk and I shared two classes: advanced placement English and an amusingly contrived and outdated anthropology elective. In college, I would learn that Mr. Serrell's lectures were essentially nineteenth-century parlor tales. But he had aced everyone for twelve years, and seniors scrambled to enroll. By the middle of the second week, we knew that this was not only an easy A but a divergent fifty-minute science-fiction flick. Several students resented him for blatantly lying, a few others hated his caustic discipline techniques (gum chewing, note passing, chatting—even an overly zealous challenge to his authority—could result in the two or three F's and D's he distributed at the end of every semester), but most of us felt a certain pity, if not empathy, for this aging high school teacher who apparently refused to read the exams we turned in. We took our A's and enjoyed his theatrical posturing and graduated with the legitimate points intact, carefully sifted from the debris. Dirkyon Patrick and Jennifer Shapiro. I ended up looking at the back of his head the entire year, our English course included.

Ms. Thompson began each inquisition with "In terms of the literature you read last night..." She'd ignore every raised hand until she had finished staring down the unprepared. Then she'd select the student least likely to respond intelligently to her question. Since I sat behind Dirk, I anguished over the expression on his face as Ms. Thompson dissected my answers. Not one of us was ever "right." But I received an A average, despite her red marks scattered throughout my every essay. "Verbosity!" she first declared. I looked up the word that evening in my parents' OED. Then she accused me of imitating Hemingway. But the A's kept coming, so I whittled every essay to fewer than four pages and avoided adjectives. Dirk and I would exchange glances as we left and occasionally brief each other on our grades.

Dirk and I graduated in May with only these scattered encounters. But our overall GPAs plus our SAT scores qualified us both for acceptance into the University of Texas at Austin. We snatched our scholarships and headed inland. Only a few of us didn't sink into debt for an education.

Only one of my friends, Stephanie, also went to U.T. We made the most of it those first few months. I was so bogged down with fifteen hours of dull required courses (calculus, symbolic logic, more French) and other freshman courses (sociology, English, trigonometry, history and government 301), that I had time for only one friend.

Not that I didn't meet people. I reviewed for psychology midterms with Michael, whose girlfriend had just left him for another guy. My flirtations were politely disregarded. He seldom washed his hair or shaved, and he wore Goodwill pants cut off jaggedly above the knee. It didn't take long for me to realize that Michael's style was no more original than his name. By the end of my first year, half the guys on campus dressed like he did and used rent money to get black designs tattooed on the backs of their calves or around their biceps. Along with the disintegration of my attraction to these clones, I began to notice that I was no longer in the majority: Jewish law forbids tattoos. A person cannot even be buried in a Jewish cemetery if she has any. I know a Jewish dancer who now has five tattoos. Her parents beg her to let them pay for skin grafts.

I was sitting outside the psychology building, watching the Austin boys sun themselves on the lawn, when Dirk walked up behind me.

"Hey, Jennifer. How are finals coming?"

"French stinks."

"I placed out of it. Spanish, German, and Italian too."

"So no more language credits for you."

"Nope," he smiled. "After a French literature course, my language requirements will be filled and the Spanish, German, and Italian credits will count as electives. The school considers English my second language, so I was free to pay my forty dollars for each test. Cheaper than a semester of any class."

"They know you're Dutch," I protested.

"So I couldn't take a placement test for it if one existed."

"No. I mean they know you've been speaking all those languages for years." Most Hollanders are, by commercial necessity, multilingual.

"Yeah, but they have too many of us to shuffle through to make exceptions for Mexican Americans who have spent five years in Japan or freshmen from European ports."

"You must feel lucky to have begun studying so many languages when you were in elementary school," I said, attempting to hide my envy.

"It was a regimen," he said.

I'd be nodding through geology class in about fifteen minutes. Three years of casual flirting suddenly struck me as a drag. "Why not come over and help me? *S'il vous plaît?*"

Dirk laughed, his smile swerving across his face in

pleasure and amusement. "Not the library?"

"Too sterile."

"In Amsterdam, we always go out in groups," he stammered.

"Really, " I replied, hoping to sound sage.

"Dating," he continued, "is reserved among Europeans for serious relationships."

"Dating is two people hanging out alone?"

"Right."

Paranoia swarmed through my head. Had I proposed marriage?

"But since I'm now an American, and we seem to be living in the States, I think a date would be appropriate." Never before had I set up a date with a guy who acknowledged the socialization as anything except "hanging out." A date. How endearing.

I couldn't help myself. "Have you ever been on a date?"

He began tightening the laces on his Converse All Stars unnecessarily. "Of course, " he answered nonchalantly.

I knew I may as well have asked whether he'd ever fucked a girl up the ass. "See you at my place at nine."

"Where do you live?

"I'm listed," I called as I hurried across campus to Pharish Hall.

Dirk rapped on my door and stood under the porch light the way people stand in elevators. We exchanged mandatory greetings, I brewed coffee, and we spread the French books across the table.

"Do you know any other languages?" he asked.

"Hebrew, some Yiddish."

"Yiddish and German. Let's go."

"What?"

"Don't be closed-minded. Just try this."

I had no idea what I was trying or why, but I didn't want him to think I was unadventurous. "You go first, " I insisted.

"Auslander."

"Oyslender," I responded.

"See what I'm getting at?" Dirk asked, waiting for some revelation from me. So we'd translated *foreigner* from German to Yiddish. I was taking French. "Try one," he commanded, as if this were more than a game. Was this the way Europeans got to know each other?

"Okay," I agreed. It had been a while since I'd run into anyone who spoke Yiddish, so coming up with a word almost stumped me. I paused, and then almost shouted, *"Loybn."* To praise. Couldn't have gotten by without that one.

"Loben," he answered. Then, *"Gelehrte."*

"Gelernter," I answered. He knew I'd know *scholar.* "Well. We've got Yiddish/German cognates." I tried not to sound exasperated.

"And English is about seventy percent French and thirty percent German. The German derivative is reserved for the crude while the French one tends to be brought out for polite occasions. Take cows in the pasture: *kuh* in German. After beef is placed on the dining-room table: *boeuf* in French. So knowing English as well as having exposure to a language as similar to German as Yiddish should make the vocabulary rather easy."

He stood and looked at the unopened books. "I'd better be leaving."

"You have an appointment?"

Dirk's face deepened several levels in ruddiness; then he started to laugh. He giggled at first, then looked at me until I started to smile and eventually laughed with him. He collapsed on the sofa. "You don't want me to leave. I mean, I thought after a brief lesson, it would only be polite, all things considered, for me to leave."

I rolled my eyes and tried to quit laughing. "What's that supposed to mean? 'All things considered'?"

"Nothing. It's just that, you are Jewish, right? Shapiro?"

"I'm Jewish, " I replied, wanting to sound calm. No one had ever asked me if I was Jewish. No one had ever excused himself because of my religion. He was still laughing, though, so I kept smiling.

"I can stay?"

"Why couldn't you?"

"Because I'm Catholic."

"Are you a priest?"

"I just thought that you'd want me to go after we studied."

"Because I'm Jewish?"

"Yeah," he said flatly. I laughed until I started to hiccup.

"My parents didn't let me hang out with Jews," Dirk said lamely. "As a matter of course, they insisted that they weren't racist. They never established friendships with Catholics who weren't prejudiced. But we aren't all like that."

"Obviously not." He was here. Who was I to hold his parents against him? My grandparents wouldn't have *goyim* in the house. Both my grandmothers bled their own meat to make it fit for human consumption and admonished my mother for trusting the kosher deli.

"So." I tried to sound casual. "Your impressions of us?"

He turned his head and answered, "The stereotypical Jewish nose gets me hard."

Jesus. If only my Jewish girlfriends who'd had rhinoplasty the day they turned sixteen could hear this. Of those who had "stereotypical" Jewish noses, over half had splurged on surgery. Stephanie had the procedure performed twice. It was sort of a status symbol. Unlike my mother or my brothers, I have a long, elegant nose, thin and perfectly straight: my father's nose. He would never have paid for a nose job, and he'd threatened when I was only thirteen to disinherit me if I ever so much as asked.

"Do I have a 'stereotypical' Jewish nose?" I pressed. I could see his cock twitching beneath his jeans.

"Yeah." Dirk crossed his legs uncomfortably.

"What else?"

"I envy a lot of Jewish values—like preserving a cultural tradition thousands of years old."

"Any culture's sustenance relies on observing its traditions," I conceded, "but we aren't museum curators; the culture is dynamic." I felt like a professor.

"Take the emphasis on education," he continued. I did sound like a professor. "Most Jews I've met have struck me as intelligent, and that knowledge has the flavor of effort to it."

I couldn't argue. I knew some exceptions, but very few. Most of our grandfathers had worked menial jobs while our grandmothers vigilantly checked their children's homework so that our parents could attend the best colleges, become the sort of sons and daughters whom their parents could boast about to their friends. My own father was an anesthesiologist and my mother was a prosecutor. I had received a merit scholarship, but I still felt the crushing pressure to *make something of myself.*

"And?" I prompted.

"Aren't most Jews politically liberal?"

"Groups that have been oppressed swing left, don't they?"

"Yes." Dirk clearly didn't want to discuss racism or genocide. I didn't either; I'd held out against the Jewish suffering for twenty years, witnessed the constant anxiety that could render my grandparents hysterical, let slide my mother's worried litany of watch-outs and what-ifs. I would not bang my head against the Wailing Wall.

"So you like my nose?"

"It's gorgeous. Like your hair and your skin." My hair is straight, shiny, and black. Very thick. My skin is olive-toned. I realized that I must seem extraordinarily exotic to a man who'd spent most of his life in Holland. "You know I've had a thing for you for years," he said, suddenly bold.

It was my turn to blush. "I know."

"Can I have something to drink?" Dirk asked nervously.

"Right this way." He followed me into the kitchen, the room I constantly explained to Christians or defended to Jews. The latter had seen their escape into academia as the perfect time to disregard the kosher dietary laws. They claimed the rules inhibited and repressed them. But how could observing the regulations of a religion suffocate a person if she had chosen to observe them? After all, I had only to declare myself an atheist or convert to some other religion to eat all the *Cordon Bleu* I could hold.

"You have two sets of everything."

"You've never been in a kosher kitchen?" I asked, incredulous; he had, after all, lived in Meyercurve. "The dairy utensils and pots are on the right, the meat things are on the left. But you just need a glass."

"Which one?" he asked.

"Any. Who drinks meat?"

Dirk got a soda from the refrigerator. He pressed the unopened can against my nipple, watching my reaction. This caught me off guard; I'd expected him to kiss me. Then he opened the can and pinched my other nipple until it too was hard. "You have great tits," he said and drank some Pepsi.

"I know." My tits are full and not yet affected by gravity. I never wear a bra, because I love for men to stare at them. Sometimes, when a guy sucks them and plays with them for a long time, I come just from that. I've learned to keep quiet, because they'd think I was faking it. I tried to keep still as Dirk pinched them through my T-shirt. He set down the soda and ran his hand under my skirt and over my panties. "Want me to make you wetter?" he asked.

The question was rhetorical. He pushed my shirt up over my tits and licked each nipple briskly as he massaged both my tits with his hands. He sucked my nipples until I had to brace myself against the kitchen sink. He ran his hand lightly over my panties again and said, "That's better. I need you dripping. Tell me, do Jewish women take it up the ass?"

"It's been known to happen." He placed me on top of the kitchen table and pulled off my skirt and underwear. He left my shirt pushed over my tits. He sat down slowly in a folding chair, spread open my labia, and licked my clit very gently. Every time I pressed my pelvis toward his mouth, he'd hold down my hips. Dirk kept me on the verge of climax for half an hour.

He unzipped his fly, slid his cock into my pussy and moaned, but he didn't repeat the thrust. Instead, he withdrew and sank his slippery cock into my asshole. I wanted it so bad by then that I didn't tense up at all. I held up a tit with each hand and pinched my nipples. If he didn't lose it, I might come from his cock up my ass and my agile fingers grasping my nipples.

"That's exquisite," he said, as he deepened his thrusts. "Don't stop playing with your tits." I hadn't intended to. "I'll take care of your pussy." I was hoping he would.

He pounded against my ass a few more times, staring at my fingers on my tits. Then he slowed to an easy, relaxed motion and ran his fingers over my inner lips, then sank them into my pussy. I spread my legs farther apart and he found my G-spot. I groaned.

"There it is," he said. He massaged my clitoris. "Aren't you worked up."

He fucked my ass and explored my pussy with one hand while he ran several fingers of his other hand over my clit. He teased, changing style, first gliding quickly over it and then flicking or massaging. I felt his cock twitch and grow even larger. I knew he was going to come soon when he asked, "What do you prefer?"

Such timing. "Rub it, in circles." He did, his fingers firm and steady, keeping exact time with his left hand and his hips. "Yeah."

"That's good. Perfect. Come for me, Jennifer," he implored. I find that a man talking to me in bed is either distracting or extremely sexy. Dirk's attention made my pelvis lurch forward, and I pressed my clit even harder against his strong fingers. "That's it," he whispered, staying with my clit even as he began jabbing his fingers into my G-spot and increasing the speed of his fucking. My pussy contracted violently, and come poured onto his hands. "Again," he insisted. After I'd come twice, Dirk freed his hands and said apologetically, "I can't hold back any longer." He braced one hand against the kitchen table while he held my thigh with the other.

"No need for apologies," I assured him. He grinned, caught being falsely modest, then started to fuck me. I realized that up until then he'd only been practicing. He left a souvenir: a ring of his fingerprints on my thigh.

His fingerprints were still visible the next morning. I admired his handiwork, then brewed some coffee and settled onto the sofa with my vocabulary notes. As soon as I got comfortable, the phone rang. I didn't answer it: that's why I'd bought a machine.

"Hi...? It's Dirk. Uh, call me when you get—"

"Just getting out of the shower, " I said reflexively as I turned off the machine.

"I thought you were the call-screening type."

"Okay. I'm reviewing vocabulary. I mean, I'm about to."

"Look up *le nez*," he told me.

"*Noz*," I confirmed in Yiddish.

Dirk laughed. "Then I don't need to translate *nase* from German."

"Not unless you're the type to look down your nose at the novice," I replied. I was beginning to wonder if our relationship was to consist primarily of trading translations when suddenly Dirk said, "Wanna go out tonight?"

I breathed a relieved "yes," and then added dryly, "*Ja. Oui. Kein.*"

Israeli Personal Ads

Actual personal ads which appeared in Israeli newspapers (taken from the Internet).

Nice Jewish guy, 38. No skeletons. No baggage. No personality.

Sincere rabbinical student, 27. Enjoys Yom Kippur, Tisha B'av, Taanis Esther, Tzom Gedaliah, Asarah B'Teves, Shiva Asar Tammuz. Seeks companion for living life in the "fast" lane.

Jewish male, 34, very successful, smart, independent, self-made. Looking for girl whose father will hire me.

Jewish businessman, 49, manufactures Sabbath candles, Chanukah candles, *havdallah* candles, Yahrzeit candles. Seeks nonsmoker.

I've had it all: herpes, syphilis, gonorrhea, chlamydia, and four of the ten plagues. Now I'm ready to settle down. So where are all the nice Jewish men hiding?

I get too hungry for *Diva* at 8. I love *The Phantom* and never come late. Won't dish the dirt 'cause it's housework I hate. That's why the lady is a JAP.

I am a sensitive Jewish prince whom you can open your heart to. Share your innermost thoughts and deepest secrets. Confide in me. I'll understand your insecurities. No fatties, please.

Eh, *shalom aleichem*. So maybe you want to meet me, although all right, you probably don't. *Nu*, so if you change your mind, maybe *epess* you'll write me, but if not, it's okay, I understand.

Divorced Jewish man, seeks partner to attend *shul* with, light *Shabbos* candles, celebrate holidays, build *sukkah* together, attend *brisses, bar mitzvahs*. Religion not important.

Couch potato *latke*, in search of the right applesauce. Let's try it for eight days. Who knows?

Are you the girl I spoke with at the *kiddush* after *shul* last week? You excused yourself to get more horseradish for your *gefilte* fish, but you never returned. How can I contact you again? (I was the one with the *cholent* stain on my tie).

80-year-old bubbe, no assets, seeks handsome, virile Jewish male, under 35. Object matrimony. I can dream, can't I?

Agnostic dyslexic insomniac male, seeks similar female to stay up all night to discuss whether or not there really is a Dog.

All my friends are doing it, and quite frankly, I feel left out. Jewish woman, 37, never married. Seeks divorce.

Attractive Jewish woman, 35, college graduate, seeks success-ful Jewish Prince Charming to get me out of my parents' house.

Boychik seeking girlchik.

Tumtumchik seeking androgynuschik.

Businessman, 51, manufactures Jewish novelty items: *chai* chairs, *chai*-fi stereos, *chai*ball glasses, *chai* jump equipment. Seeks woman with *chai* standards.

Classy carrot seeking sugar daddy to make *tzimmes* together. Prunes need not apply.

Conservative rabbi, 45, I count women for the *minyan* and call them up to the Torah. Seeking female to make *aliyah*.

Desperately seeking *shmoozing*! Retired senior citizen desires female companion 70+ for *kvetching, kvelling, krechtzing*. Under 30 is also OK.

Divorced? Looking for someone to play with? Sign on with us, the New York Gets. Games all season. Switch hitters welcome.

I enjoy long walks, candlelight dinners, sailing, travel to Europe, and I think this ad should be in *New York Magazine* instead. Sorry.

If I were sour cream and you were a *blintze*, what kind of filling would you have? Single Jewish woman, loves to cook, wants to satisfy your appetite.

If you can't stand the heat, get out of the *blech. Heimishe balabusta* ,39, will cook you such a *tzimme*s. Hurry, it's getting cold.

Israeli professor, 41, with 18 years of teaching in my behind. Looking for American-born woman who speaks English very good.

Israeli woman, 28, works behind falafel counter in pizza shop, looking for Jewish man with sense of humus.

Jewish man, watches TV on Friday night with time clock, eats fish at nonkosher restaurants, doesn't wear *yarmulke* at work. Modern Orthodox.

Jewish Princess, 28, seeks successful businessman of any major Jewish denomination: hundreds, fifties, twenties.

Looking for a great husband? "Mr. Dependable," always there for you. A faithful companion at all times. Your salvation in any emergency. No Saturday or holiday calls, please.

Mama's boy from Brooklyn, seeks wife willing to suffer abuse from my mommy.

Matzo supplier, 53, seeks cloth bag manufacturer. Let's play "Hide the *Afikomen*."

Orthodox woman with get, seeks man who got get, or can get get. Get it? I'll show you mine if you show me yours.

Professional Jewish athlete, winner of Davis Cup, America Cup, Stanley Cup. Seeking non-Jewish woman. Goyishe Cup.

Single, attractive, successful, self-absorbed woman, 34, seeks to save money by spending yours.

Staunch Jewish feminist, wears *tzitzis*, seeking male who will accept my independence, although you probably will not. Oh, just forget it.

Successful orthodox diamond cutter. Both Shea and Yankee Stadium. No *Shabbos* games. Will not mow lawn during *s'firah*. Seeking wife.

What's a *menorah* without its *shammes*? Available Jewish woman, 37, seeks man to light her fire.

Worried about in-law meddling? I'm an orphan! Write.

Yeshiva bochur, Torah scholar, long beard, *payos*. Seeks same in woman.

Yeshiva graduate, 38, handsum, carring, sinsere. Wood make gud huzband. Seeks frum girl with publick schul background to help me with my speling.

Your place or mine? Divorced man, 42, with *fleishig* dishes only. Seeking woman with nice *milchig* set. Object macaroni.

From *He, She and It*

Marge Piercy

He came so quietly she did not hear him until he was in the room. He stood by the window. "Shira?"

She felt closer to fright than to desire. Her heart was pounding, but in her mind was the idea that it was time to treat him as a person, fully, because he was nothing less; she knew, too, that she was choosing to try sex with him because when she was with him, she did not think of Gadi. He seemed able to fill all available mental space. In the intervening years, only her child had done that, her lost child. She sat up in bed. "Come."

He paused with his hand on the bedside table. "You wish it to stay dark?"

"Yes. Not because I find you ugly, but because I don't want Malkah to wake and see the light. She often has insomnia."

"Shira, why did you change your mind? Is it because I cleared the Base of danger? For Malkah?"

"Don't ask silly questions. I'm doing it because I want to."

He tore off his few garments, letting them fall, and slid

between the sheets. She wondered exactly what one did with a cyborg. She had waded through gigabytes of material on his hardware, but she was still confused. Could one kiss a cyborg? Would not his mouth be dry as a can opener? It was not. His lips were soft on hers. His tongue was a little smoother than a human tongue but moist. Everything was smoother, more regular, more nearly perfect. The skin of his back was not like the skin of other men she had been with, for always there were abrasions, pimples, scars, irregularities. His skin was sleek as a woman's but drier to the touch, without the pillow of subcutaneous fat that made it fun to hug Malkah, for instance.

"Shira, I can feel that you're tense," he said very softly.

"I'm not tremendously sophisticated or experienced. Even if you were human, I'd be nervous. To lie down with a man always feels risky."

"But I can't give you a disease or make you pregnant. I would never hurt you." Lightly, gently he stroked her back.

"You're strong enough to do so inadvertently, the way a person can hurt a baby or a bird."

"I control my movements far more exactly than any human does. I'm machined and programmed to demanding specifications. I would never hurt you, I could never hurt you. Believe that."

She smiled against his shoulder. "That would make you different indeed from any man I've known."

"Then know me, Shira. Let me know you. It's all we can do together. We can't get married or have children or run off together. All I can bring you are brain and body during the times I am not required elsewhere in acts of what I'm told is necessary violence." He tugged gently at the fine cloth of her nightgown. "Can we take this off?"

The nightgown went flying across the room and settled with a little sigh of its own on the floorboards. Moonshine lit the room faintly. His hands drifted over her lightly, lightly in wide and then narrowing circles, on her back, her breasts, her belly. He touched her as if he had all the time in the world. Of course he did not experience bodily fatigue; his desire was not based in any physical pressure; he did not sleep. He caressed her as if he could do so all night, and probably he could. She still felt watchful, wary, but her flesh woke independently of her brain, stretched, came to life, brushed into electrical response. Her back arched to his palm, her breast slipped forward into his hand. He obviously liked to be touched, to be caressed, but she did not sense that any particular part seemed more sensitive than any other, although she was too shy to touch his genitals yet. Her breath came quickly, but his did not. Yet he concentrated on her with a total intensity that in itself was absolutely exciting. It was not passion as she had known it in men: it was a passionately intense attention, sharpened by extraordinary skill in the use of his hands and mouth. Raw silk, she thought, warm in the sun. Sinuous as a cat, as the wind. She writhed against him.

Time resumed when his hand slipped between her thighs. She realized she had not had a conscious thought in…She had been outside time. And she was the one who had moved his hand downward. She had been kissing him, writhing against him, her mind doused like the *havdalah* candle that was put out in sweet sacramental wine, the candle braided as their bodies were intertwined. Who would have expected him to be so…graceful, precise, catlike in bed? Never had she lost self-consciousness like that with Josh, never, not with the lover she had tried after him or with anyone at all since Gadi.

He touched her, and then he parted her thighs and went down on her. She had always felt a little self-conscious that way. Josh had been clumsy, and she had felt shy, as if she were asking for more than she ought to. Gadi had learned from the stimmies, but they had used it for excitement only. For a moment she felt her old awkwardness, and then she thought she need not be embarrassed with him. He did not grow fatigued. He would simply continue until stopped. She gave herself over to the sensations of being lapped until the urgency and the sense of tipping over grew so strong she was coming.

"I never came that way before," she said honestly, when she had hold of herself again. "Can you feel pleasure?"

"I experience a small discharge of my fluids from friction. It has no function other than to mimic what human males produce. The pleasure is entirely in my brain."

She smiled. "Do I rub your temples, then?"

"I can come by any kind of friction. I am not programmed to require penetration."

"But would you like to do it that way?"

"I wouldn't hurt you?"

"Let's try it."

He positioned himself on her with extreme care, keeping his weight on his arms. She wondered if he had done this before. He seemed less practiced. She was still wet, and he slid in without difficulty. She was pleased to feel that he had been made a reasonable size. She had feared a giant penis on him, and was relieved Avram had not been carried away. It would be nice to make love with him in ordinary light, she thought, as she was now extremely curious about his body.

He moved very slowly at first, until she found herself

driving up at him. He probed more quickly. She forgot to think. Her nails were digging in his back. Her pelvis was drumming against him. She had never made love quite this way. She had never been as excited except with Gadi, and then she had been too young to thrust hard. She could hear herself making noises, soft growls and groans. A path opened in her, a path into her womb. She did not worry she was taking too long, she did not even think until the last moment that she could not possibly be coming again, but she could, she was, she did.

She lay beside him in the roll of messed-up covers and pulled-loose sheets. She kept touching his cheek, his fore-arms, his buttocks. He felt to her at once like a person and a large fine toy. She could not believe what she had just experienced. Since Gadi, her sexual response had been mea-sured at best, defective, sputtering. She had considered her-self rather cold. Gadi had been the exception, and that was so long ago, her sexuality so incandescently diffuse, she felt she could have come with Gadi simply by touching thumbs or kissing.

"Oh," she said suddenly, jolted. "I fell asleep for a moment."

"I wondered if that was sleep." He stroked the hair back from her face. "I should go to the lab. In the morning tell Malkah I've cleared the Base and we must reprogram. All other work must cease until we've created new labyrinths. Now Malkah is free to build and ride and play in the Base again."

After he had left her, she wanted to think about every-thing that had happened, but the long day, the tension she had been carrying wound through her guts, the soft, gummy feeling of her body after two orgasms, all sucked her down into sleep heavy as a sinking sofa. *What have I done?* she thought, waiting for alarm to hit, but then she was floating in darkness, disembodied.

* * *

Yod paused just inside the door. "Do you mind my waking you? This is the only time I could get away. They're both asleep. Malkah is dozing on a cot in the lab, and Avram is home."

"Then we can have light." She turned on the lamp beside her bed and sat up to look at him. "I've just been having a ridiculous conversation with the house. I'm beginning to argue with it as if it were a person."

"Malkah has introduced remarkable enhancements to your house. It is, of course, by no means a comparable intelligence to the large base-sized AIs or to me, but it's unusually sophisticated and capable for a private system." He came forward and stood before her bed, his hands held out a little from his sides.

She realized he was experiencing a cyborg equivalent to shyness, uncertainty. The light reflected green off his eyes. Again in the semidark they seemed more cat's eyes than human, in spite of their warm brown color. He was holding himself visibly in check, unsure of her welcome.

She slid out of bed and extended her arms to him. "I'm glad you could get away."

Instantly she was in his arms. When he moved, he moved very quickly. He ran his hand lightly over the contours of her face, as if his fingers saw as well as his eyes. She tilted her head up and tugged his down. She was by far the more impatient, for she wanted to test her own responses. She had none of the fear she had experienced the first time, fear of his body, fear of how cold or mechanical or painful a sex act with him might prove to be. He had firm control over himself, and she was convinced he would not injure her or even inadvertently bruise her. She felt herself the sexual aggressor, in a way new and exciting to her.

His lips had that soft perfect slightly dry quality she remembered. They made her think of apricots. Their tongues twined around each other, strong as pythons. She had never been afraid of snakes. Anything that could live in the raw seemed commendable: snakes were widely admired now and their forms frequently used as a public decoration. She wanted to twist all around him as their tongues were twisting.

"Touch," she said aloud. "I've been missing touch."

"I…need to touch you. I need to be touched," he said softly. "It is more important to me than the rest."

"In that, you're like a woman." She wanted to flow over him and bite him and swallow parts of him. She wanted to pull him into every orifice of her body. It was a hard succulent wanting, new to her. It made her feel strong. It made her remember something from years and years before. Yes, the early days with Gadi. He had been a stranger, just moved to the school where she was at home, the "daughter" of a Base Overseer. From her secure high perch, she reached out to the gangly newcomer, with his fervid imagination.

"Remember, a woman helped program me. Avram is very pleased with me because I destroyed the raiders and located our enemy, and because he says I have been working like a demon. Demon's an archaic concept that puzzles me."

"It's just a phrase."

"Such comparisons with the unnatural disturb me. I didn't tell him I was working at full capacity to wear everyone out so I could come to you."

It was she who helped him undress and flung away her

nightgown, she who seized his hand and tugged him into the opened bed. The kittens fled hissing from Yod, climbed the draperies, and peered down. She realized by then that while he had begun in shyness, he had read her mood from her body language and was acquiescing. He was letting her lead. It was novel and heady. Perhaps he could enjoy her aggression, for if there was any way in which he was exactly human, it was in his lack of security in himself as love object. We all of us go about, she meant to tell him but was too occupied, wanting to be wanted but unsure why anybody should bother.

Sleek and warm against her, his body was precisely engineered, well cushioned but not a bit of waste, of excess. This time she was as active as he was, caressing him back, feeling him respond. She was surprised at how sensitive his skin appeared to be. Unquestionably he could feel the lightest touch. If he had no instincts driving him against her, he had exquisite responses. There were men who spoke of women as instruments to be played upon, as the professor of cybernetics she had taken as her lover at college (seeking to obliterate Gadi with someone his opposite, intellectual, older, a scientist) had done, but that was ego speaking. However, Yod was really a beautiful instrument of response and reaction. The slightest touch of pressure on his neck, and he understood what she wanted and gave it to her. As before but even more quickly, she came to his tongue.

Going down on him, she discovered he did not taste like a human male. There was no tang of urine or animal scent to him. She missed the biological, but certainly he was clean, the pubic hair softer than a man's. Perhaps Avram had been thinking of female pubic hair. She wondered briefly, and then she mounted him. This was her ride tonight, her action, and he gave it up to her, moving under her. She could feel him reach whatever triggered his small discharge, but she did not pause, knowing now that did not affect his erection. He drove back at her. Again she felt the second orgasm gathering in her. Perhaps she had been waiting for years. She rode on toward her orgasm and then collapsed. But even then, something in the back of her brain felt like doing it again. Theoretically. She did not want to go off to the gynecologist with a sore bladder from overdoing penetration, and she knew he had to return before he was missed.

He lay on his side facing her, touching her face with his sensitive careful fingers. "I didn't know how you would feel. If you had only been with me because I broke the ambush. If you would want me to come to you."

"Do you know now?"

"I was almost afraid tonight. I wondered if I shouldn't ask you first. Now I'm glad. That's taking a chance, isn't it? When one acts without sufficient information."

"All human acts are committed on insufficient information, Yod." She settled into a comfortable S curve, their legs layered. "I can't help wondering what you feel. Can you actually experience pleasure?"

"How can I ever know if what I call by that term is what you mean?"

"I've always wondered if what men feel is anything like what women feel."

"Not being a man, I don't know. I surmise by observation that your pleasure is more intense than mine. Mine is mental. I am programmed to seek out and value certain neural experiences, which I call pleasure."

"Then sex would be something you can ignore rather easily." She was embarrassed by his observation on the intensity of her pleasure. *Do I think,* she wondered, *that a nice girl shouldn't show her orgasms? That a good woman doesn't enjoy sex too much?*

"It isn't a physiological need. But I think my need for the coupling is more intense than yours because it means intimacy to me. Who can I possibly be close to? Avram, Malkah, and you. With anyone else I must conceal my true nature. I am acting, I am on guard."

"It's usually thought to be women who want sex for the intimacy, among humans." She stroked his hair. It was of the medium length favored by most young men in Tikva, but sleeker and more uniform in color.

"I want to know everything about you. Everything in you, of you. Why can't we link as I can link to the Base?"

"You want telepathy. It's a prominent human fantasy, usually a fantasy of women, who wish they could understand what men want and tell men what they want." *Mine,* she thought as she stroked the fine modeling of his collarbone. She was amused and offended by her sense of possession. *Because he's a machine, do I think I can own him? If anyone owns him, it's Avram, but that, too, is unjust.*

"But telepathy doesn't exist."

"Or if it does, it's elusive, an epiphenomenon that can be neither summoned nor prevented, certainly not available as a regular built-in feature of relationships." It was easy to talk to him in bed, surprisingly easy.

"If we ever had enough time to talk, we could tell each other everything we have thought and felt and known."

She was just as glad he could not read all her thoughts, especially all those about him. "Soon we'll have more time to spend together again."

The Feast of the Harvest

Ariel Hart

It was Sukkoth, the weeklong feast that celebrated the gathering of the harvest. Although Rivkah would never admit this to anyone, Sukkoth was her favorite holiday. It exalted fruitfulness, nature's bounty, and the riches of the earth, while Passover, for example, though more grandiose and dramatic, seemed to Rivkah barbaric and vindictive with its lamb's blood smeared on door posts, its plagues and pestilence. Sukkoth was autumn flowers the color of fire, woven wicker baskets heavy with juicy apples, and long tables overflowing with sweetness, from *tzimmes* to chocolate macaroons and moist honey cakes.

Sukkoth was also the time when Rivkah's quiet little world in Borough Park, Brooklyn, was transformed into a wonderland. The men, usually so dour and dark in their sad wool suits, were brightened by the bundles of wood and greenery they carried home on their shoulders. At night and sometimes early in the morning, the air was alive with the tapping of hammers and the scraping of saws, until a modest hut stood in each backyard or on the concrete balcony.

The *sukkah*, or hut, was to symbolize the Jews' years of wandering in the wilderness and their history as a people who lived by the grace of the earth's bounty. In memory of this, Rivkah's people ate all their meals in the *sukkah* during these seven holy days. And she didn't mind it one bit.

Although it was strictly forbidden for women to do such work, Rivkah's husband, Adam (a freethinking fellow within the strict confines of his religion), allowed Rivkah to assist in building their *sukkah*, despite her mother's protests. "After all, you're a Jew, too," he would say to Rivkah with a gentle, halting smile as his hand fit over hers and he showed her the proper manner in which to guide a hammerhead up and down.

Underneath her shapeless, woolen skirt, which reached beneath her knees, Rivkah was extremely aroused. The thick syrup began to flow between her legs, making her sex tingle. All she could think of was Adam's warm breath on her neck, Adam's body pressing against hers. She was sure he felt it also. Once, he fit his hands around her breasts, made tiny circles until her nipples stood out in peaks, then withdrew when his sturdy cock leaped and stirred against the cleft of her backside. They resumed working and said nothing.

Until they were preparing for bed a few hours later.

There, without warning, before the bed Rivkah's great-grandmother had rescued from Poland, Adam fell to his knees as Rivkah stood before him, pulling off her sweater. He buried his face in her woolen lap, breathing in his wife's pleasant, pungent musk, which was so undeniable it embarrassed her sometimes. Rivkah tried to drag Adam up to his feet, for she knew what would come next. "No! No!" she protested, seeing him bow before her.

We don't even kneel to pray, Rivkah thought. *And this!*

This is surely a sin.

Rivkah recalled the time years earlier when she had peered into the depths of a large, foreboding, leather-bound tome called *The Code of Jewish Law* and skipped ahead to the parts addressing marital intimacies. A husband and wife should have sex only when thinking of *ha Shem* and procreation. A man should not so much as *look* at a woman's genitalia. "Of course, he must never kiss it," the harsh black-and-white words scolded.

But there Adam was, a devoted student of the Talmud, kneeling to worship his wife's sex. Rivkah shut her eyes tightly. She felt the hem of her skirt lift and the heat of Adam's body beneath it, mingling with her own fire. With one firm rip, Rivkah's white cotton panties fell away like the petals of a daisy.

Adam nuzzled Rivkah with his nose, his mouth. He rubbed his face in her wetness. He took her tender flesh between his teeth. He burrowed his tongue into her slit, astounded at the glow it radiated. When Rivkah finally had the courage to open her eyes, she looked down to see Adam's bent frame billowing out her skirt like some mythical beast from folktales. A *dybbuk*. Her forbidden demon lover. Rivkah braced her hands on either side of Adam's head, guiding it to the proper place and steadying herself for the explosion about to occur. Her knees buckled. Her thighs trembled. That moist, pink spot between her legs throbbed and expanded, seeming to fill the room, the cracked streets outside, reaching as far as the elevated train tracks, then returning.

Rivkah sobbed quietly with joy when Adam crawled out from under her skirt, his face slick as a glazed doughnut. They undressed in silence. The front of his pants jutted out, and when he unfastened them, his prick stared expectantly at her, having burrowed out of the opening of his starched white undershorts. Sitting on the edge of the bed in her creamy full slip, Rivkah returned the favor.

Even when her husband's cock was at its hardest, the skin was still satiny to the touch. It leaped at the sensation of Rivkah's breath upon it. Without a second thought, she lapped up the diamond of pre-ejaculate at its tip. Adam shuddered.

Eating of any sort was something Rivkah liked to do with her eyes open. She enjoyed watching the rubbery head disappear beyond her lips. It pleased her to cradle the stiff flesh in her fingers and admire the handiwork of the long-dead *mohel* who had circumcised her husband so expertly when he was just eight days old and his penis no bigger than a thimble.

Offering a wordless prayer of thanks to this nameless rabbi, Rivkah took Adam into her mouth. She didn't even know if she was doing this right. But there was no one to ask. It was strictly forbidden, simply not done, nor even thought of. But Rivkah had mastered the act, and she fantasized about the times her husband would permit her to suck him off.

Sooner than she liked, Adam was squeezing her shoulders. His balls, round and ripe as plums, tightened, pulled away from her fingertips, and somehow disappeared into the cavity of his body. (She would have to remember to ask him about this phenomenon some time.) Then there was a strong, rhythmic pumping at the root of him that sent a delicious confection flowing down her throat. Often Rivkah would have to swallow twice or more to get it all.

Gradually, the pumping grew weaker and weaker, then slowly subsided. Rivkah imagined this was what it would feel like to hold a throbbing heart in her hand. To grasp the essence of life. And afterward, she and Adam slept like innocent children, their limbs tangled around each other until morning.

Yes, the Feast of the Harvest was Rivkah's favorite time of year. She and Adam had been married in the autumn, just after *Sukkoth*. Unlike for most of their sect, it hadn't been an arranged union. They had been friends all their lives. The two had grown up in narrow houses six doors apart from each other. Knowing each other was like knowing themselves. From the women's section in Temple Beth Shalom, Rivkah had studied Adam's head of sandy curls bowed in fervent prayer and watched his serious blue eyes clamp onto those staunch Hebrew characters in the Talmud as far back as she could remember. And he, in turn, was drawn to her dark, Sephardic good looks, to her quizzical eyes so black they reminded him of shadows, and to her solid, unwavering mind, which questioned everything.

When the right time came, Rivkah and Adam chose to marry, with the blessing of their parents and the entire community. Adam was a patient husband, unscathed by some of the traditions he found oppressive and unfair to women. He encouraged Rivkah to take a part-time job as an accountant at a poultry market a few blocks from their apartment. They would have children when they were ready, not because of dogma or doctrines. For that reason, Adam often spilled his seed down Rivkah's throat, onto her belly, or in the delicate chink of Rivkah's ass. *Just like Onan*, she would think. Though not foolproof, it worked for them. Anyhow, it was their only option, since it was impossible to purchase birth-control devices within the tightly knit confines of their sect, and it would have been immoral to do so anywhere else.

One year in particular, on the afternoon before that first evening of Sukkoth, Rivkah strolled down Forty-Fifth Street happy and humming quietly to herself. Mr.

Lowenstein had closed the poultry market early. Rivkah carried an armful of groceries, which she switched from hip to hip. On her trip along the gnarled sidewalks, she spied men and boys in shirtsleeves, toiling in their backyards, putting the finishing touches on their *sukkahs*. There was the smell of freshness in the air. And of roses. The last roses of the season always seemed to be the most vibrant; it was almost as though they did this on purpose because they didn't want you to forget them in the grayness of winter. The sky was a shattering, cloudless blue. Everything seemed clean and bright, despite Brooklyn's constant layer of grime. Even that was tamed.

There was a spring in Rivkah's step, which her mother took to mean that she was pregnant. (She wasn't.) The older woman was elbow-deep in carefully ground pike. Although *gefilte* fish wasn't a traditional entry in the Sukkoth menu, the Radners loved it so much that it had become their family tradition at every holiday—except, of course, Yom Kippur, when they ate nothing.

Rivkah kissed her mother on the cheek and unpacked the bag of groceries. She promised to help with the stuffed cabbage and *kreplach* as soon as she changed her clothing. She climbed the steps to her and Adam's upstairs apartment two at a time. Mrs. Radner shook her head and smiled, dreaming of dark-eyed grandchildren.

But Rivkah didn't come downstairs immediately. She was beside herself with an intense overflowing of emotion. Was it the scent of dying roses along her path? Was it the warm comfort of chicken broth bubbling on the stove with *matzo* balls light as clouds swirling on top? Was it the knowledge that her belly would soon be full with goodness almost as satisfying as her husband's seed? As Rivkah undressed, she tried to ignore the throbbing between her legs. But like the autumn roses, her sex begged to be noticed, tugging insistently on her lush, ebony pubic hairs. Rivkah was sure she was moist. And when she checked, she found that the entire seat of her panties was drenched. Even her thighs were damp.

What else could she do? Rivkah knew she wouldn't be able to concentrate for hours in the kitchen working beside her mother. The woman would surely notice her hands shaking, and then what? Rivkah locked the bedroom door. Naked, she settled down on her great-grandmother's bed. Rivkah spread her legs, as she was certain her dusty ancestor *never* did, and if so, certainly not alone.

Rivkah parted her cunt, lightly, delicately, as if not wanting to disturb anyone. But still, the wet petals of her flesh made an insolent sound, like famished lips smacking. This aroused Rivkah's lust even more. From the nightstand, she retrieved the mother-of-pearl handled mirror that had belonged to her mother-in-law, *ha Shem* rest her soul. Rivkah wedged it between her knees to examine the portion of her body Adam found so intriguing. And in the process, she caught a glimpse of her own face: flushed, wild-eyed, full of desperate desire.

Her cunt was really quite curious. Not unappealing, but odd. Parts of it were bright pink and others were like red roses at sunset. Furrowed, wrinkled, yet tight and round. The hairs were silky, long. The hole itself seemed at once daunting and welcoming. And endless. Rivkah traced it with her finger. It gulped. Out of hunger? Embarrassment? She placed one hand around her mound. She squeezed the lips together, then stretched them apart. Her palm was soaked. She sniffed it—musky, deep, like a forest—and then she licked it. Flat, sharp, clean, not unlike charcoal. She could see why Adam liked tasting it.

With the mirror propped beside her on the bed, Rivkah sought the tiny button at the top of her sex. She withdrew the hood and touched her sensitive clitoris. She thought of the time in the garden a week earlier when no one was home except Adam and herself, harvesting their bursting crop of tomatoes. She recalled how he had fed her one of the plumpest fruits. When the juice dripped down her chin, he'd licked it off, kissing her deeply. And she thought of the roses.

As Rivkah touched herself, she remembered how Adam cut her hair with the same scissors she used to cut his. He didn't insist she shave her head beneath the wig Orthodox women traditionally wore. Since no one but her husband was allowed to see her with her head uncovered, how would anyone know? Adam himself gave Rivkah a pretty, cropped haircut with his own hands. She recalled how sure and sensual his fingers felt wandering through her tingling scalp. During her most recent shearing, he nibbled at her throat and whispered, "Our women cut their hair so they will only be attractive to their husbands, *nu?*" His hands moved to her breasts. "But I ask you," he breathed, "how could any man not find you beautiful?"

At that point in her reverie, Rivkah climaxed violently, rolling from side to side on the big, old bed. Although she bit her lip to keep herself quiet, she still whimpered until the throbbing ceased and the tremors subsided.

On weak legs, Rivkah dressed in a simple cotton shift, which covered her knees and elbows. She took special care washing her hands and waited until her eyes lost that savage look. She said nothing when she joined her mother at the kitchen table and began shelling almonds for the *man-*

delbrot. Rivkah's mother looked at her and smiled, fantasizing about babies-to-be.

Soon, the house was filled with people. After temple and just before the sun set, they ate. Adam watched Rivkah with a blinding pride as she—now dressed in luxurious blue velvet—carried in a platter of fruit, nuts, and sweets. Not only was she lovely, and able to earn a living and argue the Talmud with the best of them, but she could prepare such intricate delicacies. His wife gave him pleasure in countless ways. And that was a *mitzvah,* was it not? Of course it was.

After the guests had gone and the last plates had been washed and put away in the cupboards, Adam and Rivkah went outside into the backyard. It was late, but the next day there was no work for either of them. They just stood there silently under the indigo sky with pinpricked stars and a moon so full and ripe that it looked as though you could reach out and squeeze it into a cup. They said nothing, yet expressed everything. Rivkah and Adam stood there long after Mr. Nazerman from across the street put away his violin and closed his kitchen door. They stood there after Mr. and Mrs. Radner turned off their bedroom light and after the soft snoring sounds of Mr. Radner could be heard.

Adam slipped both arms around Rivkah's waist and held her close. Her hair smelled of almonds and her skin of butter. She was a fine dish indeed, fit to be eaten, to be savored, to never be forgotten.

As Adam took her in his arms, Rivkah admired the handiwork of their *sukkah.* While others erected flimsy cardboardlike hut walls, or even sheets of plastic, her husband was a stickler for detail. It wasn't enough to simply throw a layer of straw or leafy boughs on a weak structure's roof. Adam insisted that they use real wood for the walls, or else a light woven material if the weather was especially warm. Rivkah could tell that her family was amused at this behavior, but she was especially proud of him.

Neither could recall exactly how they had ended up on the cool earth beneath the shelter of the hut, but there they were, limbs draped around each other, mouths locked in a kiss, Rivkah's blue velvet dress pushed up around her waist, revealing thick, dark stockings rolled just past the knee. Although the night was black as pitch, Adam's cock found his wife's small slit by memory. He entered her with an almost inaudible popping noise. Some might say there was no detectable foreplay, yet the entire evening had been foreplay, the entire feast of the harvest, the autumn season, the coming seven days of *Sukkoth* and *Simhat Torah* soon to follow. The rejoicing of the law. Yes, they were rejoicing of the law and the harvest, and reveling in the very essence of life itself.

Adam rocked inside Rivkah, feeling her rise and fall with a surge stronger than that of the ocean. Beneath the thatched roof of the makeshift *sukkah*. In the shadow of the el train. Beneath the shelter of the stars and the cowl of the night. Across the asphalt from Mr. Nazerman's lyrical violin. Beneath her parents' bedroom window, Rivkah and Adam celebrated the harvest in their own special way. It had probably been done in this manner many times before them, in deserts and in meadows, in cities and in concentration camps. But for them, it was new.

Exactly like Onan, Adam literally spilled his seed onto the ground. For a few moments, it glowed iridescent in the moonlight. Then it disappeared, drawn into the depths of the earth.

Rivkah and Adam tried to brush the dirt from their clothing. They thought they had done a good job of it until they awoke the next morning. A rosy-pink carpet of alyssum and impatiens had sprouted on Rivkah's dress. On the knees of Adam's trousers were dwarf marigolds and creeping phlox. And when they went downstairs to breakfast beneath the *sukkah*, they found that a patch of baby's breath had begun to grow where Adam had inadvertently planted his seed.

There it continues to grow to this very day.

From
Any Woman's Blues

Erica Jong

I see him lying on a beach somewhere along the Dalmation coast (between Dubrovnik and Split, I suppose). Above us is a corniche road cut into the limestone. It crumbles and falls away in places, like the odyssey of our lives. Below us, lapping, is the Adriatic. The beach is rocky, and we have spread blankets and towels, which are littered with snorkel gear and the remains of our peasant picnic of grapes, plums, cheese, bread, and homemade wine in a wavy green glass bottle innocent of any label. The beach is deserted and we are both naked (not nude—that more polite cousin of nakedness) in the blinding sunlight. We are greasing each other's bodies in tandem: first he does my back with infinite tenderness; then I do his. Then he does my lips, my nipples, my thighs, my knees—and then he has plunged his sweet, tousled boyish head between my knees and he is slowly licking up one side of my clitoris and down the other, darting his tongue in and out of that cavity he would like to climb back into, making me come resoundingly again and again before he will deign to pull me to my knees and fuck me brutally, almost painfully, from behind, the heat of his cock corresponding to the heat of the sun that bakes us. When we are spent, we lie in each other's arms on that rocky beach, my head in his armpit, where I smell the odor that links my menstrual cycles to the moon, his sweet sweat clinging in trembling drops to the honey-blonde ringlets in the curve of his armpit.

I can remember the curl of each hair in the sunlight, the tendency his armpit hair had to tangle in little knots—which later I would tenderly cut away with a nail scissors—the faint whorls of ashen-blonde hair around his nipples, the curve of his warm belly (not as flat as he wished it, dammit—*his* dammit, not mine), and his battering ram of a cock deceptively sweet in repose, a little rosebud listing to the left and weeping one glistening dewdrop tear.

I remember the shape of his loins, the blue vein that pulsed where his leg joined his groin, the golden hair on his calves, the shape of those calves, the length of the tendons. And then I remember a slightly funny, moth-eaten odor his mouth had—not unpleasant but hinting faintly of corruption—"the moth-eaten odor of old money," he called it (for he could also be funny in a self-mocking sort of way). I noticed that odor in the beginning and then I stopped noticing it—only to notice it again right at the end.

We drove through Yugoslavia in a tiny cheap Yugoslavian car called a Zastava—the only car we could rent. The engine must have been made of plastic, and somewhere in the mountains of Macedonia it gave up the ghost. The car puttered to a halt on a mountain road in a region of infernal factories and mines, where leathery-faced peasants in sweaty bandannas seemed to be mining lead. Of course it wasn't lead, but it hung in the sky like a grayish haze, making one think of gnomes in the lands of Oz and Ev, underground factories, and regions of infernal gloom.

Not a soul spoke English in that infernal land, and there were no garages.

"Do you have a wire coat hanger, baby?" Dart asked, looking under the hood of the car, then strutting over to me as if he wanted to be awarded the *Légion d'honneur*.

I knew better than to ask why. In fact, I didn't really *want* to know why. From my expensive leather-trimmed tapestry suitcase I produced the hanger as if I were the nurse at one of those kitchen-table abortions of my youth. I was full of admiration for his WASP knack of fixing things...I who had grown up poor in Washington Heights with Jewish men who thought that when something broke, you "called the guy"—inevitably a Polack, Irishman, or Latino, or some other member of that underclass that exists for the sole purpose of sparing Jewish men manual labor. Something about Dart's ability to fix things like throttle linkages got me hot. It seemed to have a sexual dimension.

And fix the Zastava he did. As we puttered off into the Yugoslavian sunset, I thought I had found my fixer at last: my mate, my addictive substance, my pusher, my love.

Love is the sweetest addiction. Who would not sell her soul for the dream of the two made one, for the sweetness of making love in the sunlight on an Adriatic beach with a young god whose armpits are lined with gold? I thought we were pals, partners, lovers, friends. I, who had always— even in my marriages—maintained my obsessive separateness, now let myself relax into the sweetness of coupling, the sweetness of partnership, the two who are united against a world of hostile strangers.

It must be admitted: famous women attract con men

and carpetbaggers. The sweeter men, the normal men, are shyer and hesitate to come close. So one looks around and sees a world filled with Claus Von Bulows, Chéris, and Morris Townsends, in short, a world of heiress-hunters, gigolos, and grifters. The nice men, being nice, hesitate— and in love, as in war, he who hesitates is lost.

About the Authors

Judith Arcana's work has appeared in journals and anthologies in the United States, England, Canada and Denmark, including in *Prairie Hearts, Calyx, Motherwork, BRIDGES, Passager,* and *13th Moon.* Her most recent book is *Grace Paley's Life Stories, A Literary Biography* (Univeristy of Illinois Press). She is currently working on a poetry collection.

Robin Bernstein is the author of *Terrible, Terrible!*, a Jewish feminist children's book, and the co-editor of *Generation Q,* a finalist for a Lambda Literary award. She is also an editor of *Bridges,* a journal of Jewish feminist culture and politics. Her work appears in Tristan Taormino and Jewelle Gomez's *Best Lesbian Erotica 1997* and many other anthologies. This story is excerpted from a novel in progress entitled *Tammy Wexler Needs Your Help!*

Gayle Brandeis is a writer and dancer living in Riverside, California, with her husband, Matt McGunigle, and their two children, Arin and Hannah. She is currently working on her fourth novel, and she recently completed *Fruitflesh: Living and Writing in a Woman's Body,* a body awareness and creativity guide for women writers. Her favorite bagel is Jalapeño Cheese.

Cara Bruce lives in San Francisco and is the editor of the e-zine *Venus or Vixen?* She believes in leaving some things to the imagination.

Harvest Garfinkel is an Ashkenazi/Buddhist/pagan who lives in an unhip part of the San Francisco Bay Area. She had her bat mitzvah in 1960. There were no Catholic boys at the party.

Ariel Hart is the pseudonym of a freelance writer who was born and bred and still lives in Brooklyn. Her various works have appeared in everything from *Seventeen* magazine to *Screw*.

Susanna J. Herbert is the pen name of a Nice Jewish Girl (who sometimes writes as Anaiis Juishgrrl). A TV writer/producer, her erotic fiction can be seen in *Herotica 4* and *Herotica 6*. She is dedicated to the laughter and love handed down by a matriarchy of noble Jewish foremothers.

Emma Holly writes for *Black Lace* in London and has also sold a romanterotic novella to Red Sage Publishing in the United States. She loves all sorts of erotica, especially the sort with a heart.

Erica Jong is author of over twenty-two novels and collections of poetry. The excerpt in this volume is from *Any Woman's Blues* and appears courtesy of HarperCollins.

Sarah Leder is a serious Jewish scholar and a scholarly slut. She was happy to discover that her name, Sarah, means princess in Hebrew. She envisions herself as the comedic lesbian S/M branch of *Chabad*. It is her fervent hope that her efforts might help ignite Jewish souls to burn with the fire of Torah.

Joyce Moye graduated with honors from Cornell University, and then sold furniture, worked for a food corporation, started her own interior design firm, godmothered a National Historic District into existence, and served on two local zoning hearing boards. Married, she has two children and always intended to be a writer when she grew up. At present, she is a sysop on CompuServe's Erotic Literature Forum. Her agent is shopping her two-book saga of a ménage à trois. "The Nanny of Ravenscroft" is from a work in progress.

Joan Nestle's most recent book is *A Fragile Union: New and Selected Writing* (Cleis Press, 1998). She is co-founder of the Lesbian Herstory Archives. "The Gift of Taking" is from *A Restricted Country* and appears courtesy of Firebrand Books.

Lesléa Newman is the author of many books that explore themes of being a Jew and being a lesbian, including the novel *In Every Laugh a Tear* and the short story collection *A Letter to Harvey Milk*. She is also the editor of several books of erotica, including *Pillow Talk: Lesbian Stories Between the Covers, The Femme Mystique* , and *My Lover Is a Woman: Contemporary Lesbian Love Poems*. Other recent titles include two books of humor: *Out of the Closet and Nothing to Wear* and *The Little Butch Book.*

Marge Piercy is the author of over twenty-four novels and collections of poetry. The piece that appears in this volume is from *He, She and It*, a futuristic novel set in a Jewish community, and is reprinted courtesy of Alfred A. Knopf.

Carol Queen credits her first Jewish lover with her present comfort with sex; *"L'Chaim"* is a gift to her, these many years later. Queen is the author of *Exhibitionism for the Shy*, *Real Live Nude Girl*, and the erotic novel *The Leather Daddy and the Femme*.

Stacy Reed is a writer attending graduate school at the University of Houston. She was a full-time journalist and editor for over four years, and holds an honors degree from the University of Texas at Austin. Reed's erotic fiction has been published in *First Person Sexual* as well as in *Herotica 3, 4*, and *5*. Her essay "All Stripped Off" appears in *Whores and Other Feminists*.

Elaine Starkman is co-editor with Marsha Lee Berkman of *Here I Am: Contemporary Jewish Stories from Around the World* (Jewish Publication Society, 1998) and author of *Learning to Sit in the Silence: A Journal of Caretaking* (Papier-Mache, 1993). She lives in Northern California with her reliable partner of thirty-six years. She is the mother of four adult children and three small grandsons. She teaches at Diablo Valley College part-time and writes poetry.

Claudine Taupin is the pseudonym of a Jewish writer whose work has appeared on the Web and in print publications nationwide. Claudine enjoys spending time with her husband and subverting the status quo whenever possible.

About the Editor

Marcy Sheiner is editor of *Herotica* 4, 5, and 6 (Plume; Down There Press). Her stories and essays have appeared in many anthologies and publications. She is currently working on a book called Sex for the Clueless (Citadel, 1999). Visit her web site at www.sexsense.com.

Glossary of Terms

Afikomen—piece of matzo hidden by the adults before Passover seder begins.

aliyah—ascent

Asarah B'Teves—tenth day of the month of Teves, a fast day

babka—Russian/Polish coffee cake

balabusta—an immaculate housewife

bashert—fate

bentsch licht—a blessing for light, said when lighting candles

blech—yuck!

bochur—young man

bris—circumcision ceremony

chai—life

challah—a braided egg bread

Chanukah—Festival of lights

cholent—a simmering stew of meat, beans and/or vegetables

chuppah—wedding canopy

dayenu—literally "it would have been enough," said in gratitude, from a Passover song

dybbuk—a spirit that possesses a living person

eppes—eat

Erev Shabbat—the afternoon before the Sabbath

feh—Phooey!

fleishig—of the flesh. Refers to food that is meat as opposed to milk/dairy; dishes used for meat

get—divorce document

Gottenyu—Dear God!

goy—non-Jew

goyim— non-Jews, plural of goy

goyische— non-Jewish

Gut Shabbas—Good Sabbath

Halacha—Jewish law

ha Shem—literally, "the name"; common usage for God.

havdallah—division, separation. Also the ceremony at the end of the Sabbath to mark the beginning of the work week.

heimische—home-like; real people, as opposed to phony

kiddush—prayer said over wine at the beginning of a holiday

krechtz—sigh or groan

kreplach—dumplings filled with meat or cheese, boiled or fried kvell—to take extreme pride or pleasure in

kvetch—complain

latke—pancake

L'Chaim—To life!

macher—big shot

maidl, maideleh—young girl

matzo, matzah—flat cracker; unleavened bread

meshugeneh—crazy; crazy person

mitzvah—commandment; good deed

menorah—candleholder used on Chanukah

mandelbrot—almond cake

milchig—foods that contain dairy; dishes used for dairy

minyan—quorum for prayer (traditionally, ten adult men)

mohel—one who performs circumcision

nosh—snack

nu—"Well?" "So?" Used for emphasis

payos—earlocks, the ringlets that grow from a man's sideburns

Pesach— Passover

putz—penis. Slang for jerk, as in "dick."

schlong—penis

schmaltz—melted animal fat; dramatically sentimental

schmuck—prick, literally and figuratively

Shabbos, Shabbat—the Jewish Sabbath (sundown Friday to sundown Saturday)

Shaddai—related to holiness

shah—"Quiet!"

Shalom Aleichem—Peace

Shaygetz—non-Jewish man

shammes—religious servant; the middle "helper" candle used to light the other Chanukah candles

Shekkina—divine presence (feminine)

shiksa—non-Jewish woman

shul—a synagogue; Jewish temple

Shiva Asar Tammuz—seventeenth of the month of Tommuz, another fast day

Simhat Torah—rejoicing with the Torah

Sukkoth—seven-day holiday in the fall celebrating the harvest

Taaris Esther—Askhenazaic pronunciation of Hebrew

takeh—"like, really man!"

Talmud—The sixty-three-book commentaries on the Torah

Torah—the text of the five books of Moses; more generally, the entire range of Jewish knowledge

trayf—not kosher

tuchus—ass

tzimmes—slow-cooking casserole of fruit, meat and vegetables

vey iss mir—"woe is me!"

vilde chayah—wild beast, wild woman

Yahrzeit—anniversary of a death

yarmulke—a small round cap worn in shul and worn by religious Jews at all times

yenta—originally, matchmaker; commonly, a gossipy person

Yiddishkite—Jewishness, usually referring to Askhenazaic Jewish culture, not religion

Yom Kippur—Day of atonement, the highest of Jewish Holy Days

zaftig—literally, "juicy," though often used as a euphemism for fat

Copyright notices and reprint permissions

Cleis Press

The steamiest, most thought-provoking erotic literature!
You'll find these and other books from Cleis Press
at your local bookseller — and on our web site!
www.cleispress.com

The Oy of Sex: Jewish Women
Write Erotica
edited by Marcy Sheiner.
$14.95. ISBN: 1-57344-083-3

Friday The Rabbi Wore Lace:
Jewish Lesbian Erotica
edited by Karen X Tulchinsky.
$14.95. ISBN: 1-57344-041-8

Best Lesbian Erotica 1999
Tristan Taormino, Series Editor.
Selected and introduced by Chrystos.
$14.95. ISBN: 1-57344-049-3

Best Gay Erotica 1999
Richard Labonté, Series Editor.
Selected and introduced
by Felice Picano.
$14.95. ISBN: 1-57344-048-5

Annie Sprinkle: Post Porn Modernist:
My Twenty-Five Years as a
Multimedia Whore
by Annie Sprinkle.
$24.95. ISBN: 1-57344-039-6

Queer PAPI Porn: Gay Asian Erotica
edited by Joël B. Tan.
$14.95. ISBN: 1-57344-038-8

The Leather Daddy and the Femme:
An Erotic Novel
by Carol Queen.
$14.00. ISBN: 1-57344-037-X

Switch Hitters: Lesbians Write Gay
Male Erotica & Gay Men Write
Lesbian Erotica
edited by Carol Queen and
Lawrence Schimel.
$12.95. ISBN: 1-57344-022-1

AVAILABLE AT YOUR
FAVORITE BOOKSTORE &
FROM CLEIS PRESS

How to Order
- **Phone:** 1-800-780-2279 or
  (415) 575-4700
  Monday - Friday, 9 am - 5 pm
  Pacific Standard Time
- **Fax:** (415) 575-4705
- **Mail: Cleis Press**
  P.O. Box 14684, San Francisco,
  California 94114
- **E-mail:** Cleis@aol.com
www.cleispress.com

Since 1980, Cleis Press has published provocative, smart books — for girlfriends of all genders! Cleis Press books are easy to find at your favorite bookstore — or direct from us! We welcome your order and will ship your books as quickly as possible. Individual orders must be prepaid (U.S. dollars only). Please add 15% shipping. CA residents add 8.5% sales tax. MasterCard and Visa orders: include account number, exp. date, and signature.